MISADVENTURES

OF A

BIKER

MISADVENTURES

OF A

BIKER

BY
SCOTT HILDRETH

WATERHOUSE PRESS

Derek "The Bone" Hildreth sat across from me and waited patiently for me to finish this novel so we could spend some time together during his last Christmas break from college. That time never arrived. As always, my work took precedence. For his sacrifice, I must dedicate this book to him. Derek, this one's for you.

CHAPTER ONE

D E V I N

I didn't regret the actions of my past. Not one. Nevertheless, I couldn't help but wonder how different my life could have been if I hadn't spent the past ninety-seven months in federal prison.

Being incarcerated hadn't changed my appearance. On the surface, I was the same person. And when I walked beyond the razor wire–topped fence that separated the institution from the free world, I was sure my life would begin where it left off.

I was mistaken. Now labeled a criminal, finding a place that would employ me was proving to be difficult, if not impossible. With a pool of law-abiding citizens to choose from, it seemed I provided potential employers with no good reason to select me. Each company gave a different version of the same apology.

We're sorry, Mr. Wallace. We've decided to go another route.

I had until Monday to find a job. If I failed to do so, my parole officer would send US Marshals to hunt me down and drag me back to prison. Considering it was Friday, I was willing to accept the first position someone offered.

Standing in front of potential place of employment

number twenty-seven, I checked my reflection in the tinted-glass door. My long-sleeved shirt hid most of my tattoos. The ones on my hands, knuckles, and the base of my neck were impossible to conceal. Hoping whoever conducted the interview was open-minded, I pushed the door open and stepped inside.

I stopped dead in my tracks. Floor-to-ceiling windows were in every direction. Long planks of gray hardwood flooring gave the space a feeling of endlessness.

Twenty feet away, a curved reception desk acted as the foyer's centerpiece. The massive section of seamless blond wood was fitted with a white Carrara marble countertop. Gray veins trailed through the stone in every direction.

Two identical waiting areas flanked the enormous desk. Decorated with brightly colored contemporary furnishings, they appeared like everything else.

Clinical.

Beyond the atrium, a V-shaped wall was centered behind the reception area. Following the theme of the waiting areas, each leg of the wall shared identical attributes—a corridor with two large pieces of abstract art on either side.

There wasn't a soul within sight. Muffled voices came from each of the two corridors. I sauntered to the receptionist's desk and peered over the massive slab of stone. An ergonomic mesh office chair, a telephone, and a computer monitor were all that cluttered the twenty-foot-wide space.

I cleared my throat.

The sound of distant voices continued.

I rapped my knuckles against the wooden edge of the desk. A hollow thud echoed throughout the lobby.

Five minutes passed. I was fractionally more versed on

the intricacies of modern art but no closer to landing a job. Left with no alternative but to take a stroll down one of the hallways and hope for the best, I chose the corridor on the left.

I paused beside the first open door. I waited while a woman spoke on the phone. As soon as she hung up, I stepped into the doorway. An attractive thirty-something brunette was seated at her desk, carefully tapping the tips of her fingers against the screen of her phone. The white sleeveless dress she wore accentuated her well-toned arms. She set her phone aside and looked up. Upon seeing me, she gasped.

"Oh my God." She covered her mouth with her hands. "You scared the crap out of me."

I shrugged apologetically. "Sorry."

She lowered her hands. "Are you with Neeson?"

"Pardon me?"

"Neeson-Frye," she said, flashing a set of snow-white teeth. "The decorator?"

I shook my head. "No, I'm not. Are you Teddi?"

"Teddi?" She stood. "I'm sorry, she's out." She gave me a quick once-over. "Is there something I can help you with?"

She had olive skin and the figure of an athlete. Her wavy hair was parted in the middle and swept away from her face. Caramel tendrils blended well with what I expected was her natural color, a chocolaty brown. Her full lips were parted, and the corners of her mouth were turned up slightly. There was only one way to describe her.

Breathtakingly attractive.

"A friend sent me," I replied, meeting her gaze. "He saw Teddi at the bank yesterday. She told him she needed to hire a receptionist."

Her face washed with confusion. "You're applying for the receptionist position?"

"I am," I replied. My tone lacked the enthusiasm I hoped to convey. "I'm pretty excited about it, too."

She paraded around the corner of her desk and paused. She folded her arms beneath her perky breasts. "Really?"

I offered her a phony smile of reassurance. "Really."

"You don't seem very convincing."

I scowled. "I take exception to that remark."

"Oh, wow," she said. "You *are* serious."

"I'm looking for a change of pace," I said matter-of-factly.

"It's just—" She shook her head. "You don't look like a receptionist."

"What do I look like?"

She shrugged one arm. "A tattoo artist? An artist?" She looked me over good, taking a moment to study my visible tattoos. "Maybe a movie producer or something. A creative type, for sure."

"Sorry to disappoint you," I said. "But I'm just a guy who desperately needs a job."

"What's your background?"

"Construction. Four years hands-on. A little less than ten in management."

"So, you know the trade?"

"I can't pretend to know your side of it entirely, but I know every facet of construction."

"Janine's going to go nuts over your tattoos," she said, nodding at my hands. "I can't wait until she sees them."

"Who?"

"Janine." She tilted her head to the side. "She's crazy about hand tattoos. Tattoos in general, really."

"Does that mean I've got the job?"

"The position has been vacant for two weeks. We haven't

had one decent applicant. This time of year, the only people searching for work are either in school and looking for a part-time job, or they're seventy years old and hoping to supplement their social security."

Naples, Florida, had roughly twenty thousand residents in the off-season and three hundred thousand during the winter months. The city was built to support the influx of inhabitants, leaving many businesses to suffer from April to December. The reduced income during the slow months wasn't the typical business owner's only frustration. A small selection of available year-round employees was equally unnerving.

"I'm well aware," I said. "I went to high school here." I extended my hand. "I'm Devin Wallace, by the way."

"Sorry, I should have introduced myself." She shook my hand. "Katelyn Winslow. I go by Kate."

She wasn't lacking in the self-esteem department, but everyone needed reassurance from time to time that they were attractive. I gave her a quick undressing with my eyes and grinned. "I can start on Monday."

She flushed a little. "Come with me. I'll grab an employment packet."

I followed her to a large conference room. She disappeared momentarily and then returned with a manila folder. She placed it on the table beside me.

"There's an application in there, an I-9 form, and a four-page questionnaire," she said, gesturing to the folder. "It shouldn't take you long. Let me know when you're done."

The questionnaire resembled the personality profile assessment I'd taken upon entry to the Federal Bureau of Prisons. Realizing the similarities between the two tests, I answered most of the questions opposite of what I had in prison. Being independent, dominant, impatient, and analytical weren't qualities I suspected they were seeking. After completing the questionnaire, I reached for the application. The first question following my personal information was the same one that had prevented me from being hired on my twenty-six previous attempts.

Have you ever been convicted of a felony?

If I lied and got caught, it would be a one-way ticket back to the joint. If I told the truth, I wouldn't be hired. In four days, I'd be picked up by US Marshals for not complying with the conditions of my release. Under no circumstances was I going back to prison.

I stared at the question, wondering what I could do differently.

Excluding that question, I filled out the application and placed it in the folder. Hearing the *click-clack, click-clack* of an approaching pair of heels, I pushed everything aside and turned my chair toward the door.

A petite blonde stepped through the doorway and paused. The buttermilk tone of her poker-straight hair was about as credible as my personality profile responses. Massive fake boobs heaved out of the plunging neckline of her bright-yellow dress with each breath. In contrast to her age—which I guessed to be in the mid-thirties—her deep brown skin was leathery and sun-spotted from overexposure to Southwest Florida's sun.

I stood. "Teddi?"

"Janine." She looked me up and down. "Janine Bazoli."

Her Jersey accent was subtle but impossible to hide completely.

"I'm Devin," I said. "I'm applying for the receptionist's position."

"Yeah." She gave me another quick look. "So I heard."

"Out of curiosity." I turned to face her. "Are there any men in this office?"

"Including you, there's one."

"How many women?"

"Four full-time and one part-time," she replied. "That doesn't include Theresa Bianchi's skinny little ass, who uses this office to do her deals because the lying bitch doesn't have a Realtor's license."

Before I could comment, she continued.

"You can tell her I said that, too. I'd say it to her face if she was standing beside you."

Several of the men I was in prison with were from New Jersey. One thing they all had in common was that their attitudes preceded them. Apparently that held true with Jersey's women, as well.

"I don't know if I'll ever have the opportunity to meet her," I said. "But I'll make a mental note of what you said, just in case."

She nodded toward the folder. "Kate said all she's waiting for is for you to fill out those papers."

"She told you I have the job?" I asked, expressing more excitement than I intended.

"Yeah." She looked at me like I was an idiot. "I just said that."

"Pleasure to meet you." I picked up the folder. "I'm going to take this stuff to her."

I rushed past Janine and into the hallway, hoping I wasn't wrong about my interpretation of Kate. With the employment packet pinched in the web of my hand, I stepped in front of her open door.

She peered over the top of her monitor. "Oh, are you done?"

"More or less," I said. "I just had a couple of questions."

"Oh. Okay."

I stepped inside her office. "Can I ask you three personal questions?"

"Me?"

"Yes."

"Don't put too much credence in that four-page thing," she said. "We only use it to see who's suitable for management positions. It really doesn't apply to you."

"It's not that."

"Oh. Well. Sure." She draped her hair over her ears and smiled. "Ask away."

"Have you ever tried oysters on the half shell?"

"Oysters." She wrinkled her nose. "No."

"Are you married?"

She seemed offended at the question.

"This isn't a proposition or an inventory of your worth. Just play along. I've got a point to make, I promise."

"Married?" She sighed. "No."

"If you were dating someone and they really wanted you to try an oyster while you were out on a date, would you?"

"I mean. If he really wanted me to, sure."

"If you liked it, would you admit it?"

"If I did? Sure. I'm kind of a foodie, so I like it when I find new foods."

I lifted my extended index finger. "One more question."

Her brows raised. "Who's being interviewed for the job? You or me?"

"I wanted to find out who I was dealing with before I answered one of these questions."

She folded her arms over her chest. "Who are you dealing with?"

"An open-minded woman who wouldn't condemn someone for a mistake he made."

She smirked. "You've been convicted of a felony, haven't you?"

I hadn't reached a point where I was comfortable talking about it with her. Not yet, at least. But there was no avoiding the issue.

Instead of slumping my shoulders in defeat, I puffed my chest proudly. "I have."

"That's okay," she said dismissively. "I mean, as long as it wasn't for something bad."

Bad wasn't clearly defined. I mulled over my response.

Not receiving an immediate answer, her face contorted. "It wasn't bad, was it?"

"I don't think so," I replied. "I'll give you the abbreviated version."

She leaned back in her chair. "Okay."

"I was walking out of a bar, and a guy was arguing with a girl just outside the door. They were surrounded by a large group of people, so I figured it was just some drunken argument about who was going to drive home. Before I got to my motorcycle, I heard her scream. When I turned around, he had her by her coat and his hand was cocked, like he was going to hit her. I told him to let her go. He said, 'Go home, asshole. This doesn't concern you.' I guess he thought with all the people surrounding him that he was safe. Just to let him know he wasn't, I said, 'Fuck you.' Five minutes later, he was in a pile beside his car, and I was being handcuffed."

"That's it?" she asked.

"More or less."

"So, what? You spent a weekend in jail or something?"

It was time to let the cat out of the bag. I twisted my mouth to the side and arched a brow. "Eight years and a month."

"Holy crap!" Her eyes bulged. "Eight years? For a bar fight? Why?"

"When I said, 'fuck you,' one of his friends thought I said, 'fuck Jews.' He testified under oath that those were the words he heard. Because I was in a motorcycle club, and because he was Jewish, they made it a gang-related hate crime. The judge gave me eight years."

"You were in a motorcycle club?" she asked excitedly.

She was all but drooling. She seemed rather disinterested in the fact that I'd pummeled a man half to death.

I gave an affirmative nod. "Yeah."

"Like *Sons of Anarchy*?"

We made the *Sons of Anarchy* look like nuns. At my earliest convenience, I intended to return to them and to the life I left behind. They were the only family I had, and being without them was a reminder of it.

I shrugged. "More or less."

Her eyes widened. "Oh, wow."

I gave her a moment to digest everything. Staring blankly at the tattoo on my neck, she seemed to be taking it rather well.

"So, what should I do about that question?" I asked. "Is it going to be a problem?"

"That's it? You beat up a guy because he was hitting a girl?"

"In summary, that's all that happened."

She wrinkled her nose. "How bad did you beat him up?"

If I was mad enough to beat someone, they didn't get a mild ass whipping. I beat the guy within an inch of his life. I didn't think expanding on the subject was necessary. She'd undoubtedly Google me and read about it anyway.

"It was a suitable punishment for what he'd done," I said.

"Eight years." She shook her head in disbelief. "How long ago was that?"

"The fight?"

"Umm. Yeah."

"About eight years ago," I responded. "Roughly."

Her eyes widened a little more. "You *just* got out of prison?"

I nodded. "Sixteen days ago."

She looked me over. Thoroughly. Not as if she were sexually interested. It seemed to be more of an inspection, of sorts.

"I've got a few questions for you. Are you ready?"

"Sure."

"Have you ever been violent toward a woman?"

It seemed like an odd question for a job interview. I shook my head. "No."

"Arrested for domestic violence?"

"No."

"Had a PFS filed against you?"

"A what?"

"Protection from Stalking order."

I chuckled. "No."

She gave me a side-eyed look. "You know I can find out if you have."

"I haven't."

"Have you ever stolen anything from someone you knew?"

"No."

"Is this a job you can see yourself keeping?" she asked. "Or is it a stepping stone to something bigger?"

"If I like it here, I'll stay," I replied, not really knowing if the statement was completely true. I'd at least stay long enough to satisfy my parole officer.

"Check the box," she said with a nod. "Everything will be fine."

"I'm hired?"

She tried to change her grin to a stern look. "If you'll accept forty-two thousand a year as salary."

"Make it fifty thousand."

She put her hands on her hips. "Forty-six."

Considering my housing arrangement with the eighty-year-old widower I lived with, I could survive on five thousand a year. My only real concern was staying out of prison.

"Go forty-eight, and I'll agree."

"Fine," she said. "Forty-eight thousand it is."

"I don't need to see Teddi?"

"She's not here, so I'm making an executive decision. In fact, let's keep the entire you've-been-to-prison thing between you and me, okay?"

"You don't want me to tell her?"

"Not yet."

"What if she sees my application?"

"She won't."

"She might."

She grinned mischievously. "Not if I misplace it."

"So, that's it?" I asked. "I'm hired?"

She extended her hand. "Welcome to the team."

CHAPTER TWO

TEDDI

Naples had three types of homes. Those situated in gated communities, the mansions along the Gulf Coast, and everything else. My focus was selling the first two types of homes. I left the *everything else* for the remaining Realtors who spent their time scurrying to match my sales figures.

The average asking price for my homes was eight figures. Properties were typically on the market for sixty days or less, and it was common for me to obtain ten percent over ask. In the world of Southwest Florida Realtors, I was despised. In the community, men respected me, women feared me, and those who didn't know me referred to me using the word no woman wanted to be called.

"Sixty days?" I choked on my wine. "Margaret. Really? It's the off-season. You can't expect me to—"

"You've had the listing for six months, Teddi." She folded her napkin and laid it beside her half-eaten plate of ceviche. "We've got two hundred million tied up in two homes, one of which we don't need. Raymond's livid about this. He said to give you sixty more days. If the home isn't sold at that point, we'll look at other alternatives."

Other alternatives meant other listing agents. If I lost the listing, it would my first. I'd become the laughingstock of the industry. The loss would be the beginning of the end my career. I took a gulp of wine and then another. It wasn't my fault the home hadn't sold. Its continued existence on the MLS listing certainly wasn't from my lack of trying.

Six months prior, I sold Raymond and Margaret a one-hundred-and-thirty-million-dollar modern beachfront mansion. They then placed their twelve-thousand-square-foot Mediterranean home on the market for less than half that amount.

The sixty-million-dollar mansion had been crafted of imported limestone. Standing at the gated entrance, it was breathtaking. The interior, however, was plagued with massive marble columns, hand-carved dark wood ceilings with Venetian plaster inlays, imported Emperador marble that was even darker, and arched stone doorways. Short of a wealthy European couple, I could see no one accepting the dungeon-esque home in as-is condition.

I pushed my empty wineglass to the side. "See if he'll entertain a hundred and eighty days. That will give me an opportunity to direct my focus solely on European clients. I should be able to schedule viewings—"

"Sixty days," she said. "He was adamant. I'm sorry."

"What can I do, Margaret? We've known each other for what? Almost fifteen years? I sold you your first home here, right after Raymond—"

Her apologetic look hardened to one of distress. "I'm sorry."

There was clearly nothing she could do.

Fuck. Fuck. Fuckity-fuck-fuck-fuck.

I put on a smile. "I'll get my team on it."

"I want *you* on it, Teddi. I want you devoted to this sale."

"It will be my only focus," I assured her. "My team will be on it as well."

She pushed herself away from the table. "I hope this ends well. I'd certainly—" She shook her head. "The thought of a new agent is appalling."

I reached for my wine and then realized it was empty. I ogled the glass as if it were a mystery. "I couldn't agree more."

She stood. "You'll be in touch?"

Yeah, as soon as I find a filthy-rich Greek doctor.

I needed to pay for our lunch. I stood and shook her hand. "I sure will."

She turned away.

I fell into my seat and sighed. A cursory glance around the restaurant produced no one of importance. Relieved, I checked my messages on my phone.

"Did the other party leave?" the waiter asked.

"She did," I responded without looking up. "I realize it's probably on the way out, but you can forget the food. Would you bring me another glass of wine, please?"

"Forget the food, ma'am?"

I set my phone down and shifted my attention to him. "I'll pay for it, but I'm not hungry any longer. Just bring the wine, please."

He nodded. "Very well."

"On second thought," I said, "bring a bottle."

★ ★ ★

It was barely noon, and I was shitfaced. A giggle fit in the front seat of my car turned to a crying session. Incapable of driving, I swept the tears from my cheeks with the heels of my palms and called an Uber.

A ride from hell in the back seat of an un-air-conditioned car suited for an alley of clowns followed. Despite my desire to roll down the window, I couldn't find a switch anywhere. After the fifteen-minute drive to the office, the back seat of his car was drenched in ten pounds of my sweat.

The driver pulled into the parking lot. "Here you go."

We were two hundred yards from the entrance. I didn't care. I couldn't get out of the rolling sauna quick enough. I thrust my hip against the door and sucked in a lungful of Florida's muggy summer air.

I wrestled to free myself of the miniature back seat. As I wiggled through the opening sized for a starving teen, I glanced over my shoulder. "You don't know any rich blind Italians looking for a home, do you?"

"Excuse me?"

With one leg out of the car and the other close behind, my purse got stuck between the back of his seat and the front of mine. The strap yanked against my shoulder, nearly sending me tits up onto the asphalt. After an embarrassingly long struggle, I pulled it free.

He stuck his head out the window. "Is everything okay?"

"No." Stumbling to catch my balance, one of my knees buckled. I careened forward at ten times the speed my feet could move. After a dozen stutter steps, I came a screeching halt. Once I was planted firmly on my feet, I resituated my purse and shot him a glare. "It's not."

He opened his door and leaned outside. "What did you say about Italians?"

"Nothing," I said in a huff. "I'll tip you on the app."

An ocean of asphalt separated me from the entrance. Not

certain that he'd even taken me to the right place, I scoured the parking lot for a familiar vehicle. The first thing that caught my attention was a Harley-Davidson parked in the *employee* section of the lot. Assuming it was one of Neeson-Frye's decorators, I shrugged it off and began my trek to the door.

I'd lived in the area my entire life and had yet to become accustomed to Southwest Florida's ninety-seven-degree, ninety-five-percent-humidity summers. Heat rose from the parking lot in waves, each of which took my breath away. Halfway to my destination, I was drenched in sweat and my hair was a disaster.

My feet were throbbing. I couldn't see straight. With each step, my heels sank into the molten asphalt. If I continued the trek in my Christian Louboutin *So Kate* heels, I'd be *so facedown* before I reached the door.

I took off my shoes. The parking lot's blistering-hot surface was impossible to stand on. Barefoot, I clutched my shoes in my left hand and my Hermès bag in my right. I bounded across the scorching sea of black tar like a gazelle across an African savannah.

Drunk and disappointed with myself, I arrived at the entrance. The bottoms of my feet felt like I'd walked over a mile of hot embers. Exhausted, I leaned against the door and stumbled inside.

The cool air hit me like a speeding freight train. My stomach heaved. My heels clattered to the floor. Wine-soaked ceviche rose in my throat. My shoulders slumped. The floor began to spin. My purse fell at my feet with a *thud*.

I braced my hands against my knees. "Kate!" I gazed at my filthy feet. "I need help!"

I closed my eyes and begged the vomit gods to spare me.

Footsteps approached. A hand gripped my left bicep. Thankful that someone came to rescue me, I lifted my drunken head.

Tall and muscular, he towered over me like a giant. A ruggedly handsome, tattooed giant. A five-o'clock shadow peppered his chiseled jaw. I darted my eyes to his crotch. It looked like he had a Chipotle burrito shoved deep in his pocket.

"Who are you?" I cooed.

"Wallace," he replied in a baritone voice. "Devin Wallace."

I despised men, regardless of age, income bracket, or looks. Having been fucked over by one so bad it nearly landed me in bankruptcy court, I knew better than to allow myself to fall into another trap. Knowing in advance that all men were pigs allowed me to use them for their intended purpose. I wasn't interested in troubling myself with feelings, emotions, or the inconveniences that accompanied a relationship.

Men were placed on this earth to change oil, move heavy objects, forfeit their lives in pursuit of obtaining world peace, and for the sexual satisfaction of women.

Nothing else.

Considering that my car had a fresh oil change, all the new furnishings were in place, and he wasn't wearing a uniform or badge, I planned to use him for the only thing that was left.

My pickled brain couldn't seem to formulate another word, let alone a sentence. I mentally assembled a brief explanation of what I needed from him, but I couldn't lift my thick tongue. I held his brown-eyed gaze and hoped he could read my mind.

Kate stepped between us. "Oh my God," she whispered. "What happened?"

I peeled my eyes away from his and glanced in her direction. "Margaret's going to take back the listing," I blurted.

"We've got two months."

"Seever?" she asked. "The Mediterranean mansion on Gordon Drive?"

I nodded. "That's it."

She looked at my feet and then at me. "What happened?"

"With her or my feet?"

"Both."

I draped my arm over her shoulder. "Guide me to my office. I need to sit."

Stumbling to keep up with her surefooted pace, I glanced over my shoulder. The well-endowed baritone interior architect was collecting my shoes and purse from the floor. In addition to being handsome, it appeared he was a gentleman. Even so, he was a man.

Kate lowered me into my chair. I fell into it like a tranquilized hippo.

"You're trashed," she said.

I pressed my palms against my temples. "I'm so drunk." I looked around my office. "Do you have anything I can take?"

"Like what?"

"A couple dozen Xanax?"

She rolled her eyes. "There's Tylenol in the conference room."

"I need something to calm my nerves. I feel like I'm going to explode. Or puke. Maybe both."

"Where's your car?" she asked. "Please tell me you didn't drive."

"It's with the valet at Mercato." I straightened my posture the best I could. "I came here in a clown car."

"What?"

"One of those stupid little Fiats. It looked like it should be filled with clowns at a circus." I cleared my desk with a swipe of my arm. I laid my head on the cool surface. "The back seat was insufficient for anything but a toddler. It didn't have air conditioning."

"An Uber?"

"Uh-huh. It was awful."

"Why didn't you get an XL?"

"It's off-season," I said. "There weren't any."

She bent over and looked me in the eyes. "How much did you drink?"

"Two glasses of wine, and then Margaret dropped the bomb." I closed my eyes. "I had another bottle and a half after that. I had to tip the waiter a hundred bucks to let me overindulge."

"Take a nap," she said. "We can talk about it when you wake up."

"Shut the door on your way out if you don't mind," I muttered, half asleep already.

"Okay."

"Who's the sexy guy with the tattoos?" I asked, smiling at the thought of him. "An architect?"

"He's our new receptionist," she replied. "I was going to surprise you."

My head shot up off the desk. "What?"

"I hired him on Friday. You were out all day, and he was the only applicant worth hiring. You said to hire someone if they were attractive and able. He's both. He's a friend of Herb what's-his-name. The old guy you sold the place in Pelican Bay to. The big house that needed to be redone by the clubhouse. You saw him in the store the other day."

"Herb Riley?"

"Yeah. That's him."

I buried my face in my open palms and exhaled a long breath. If we employed Mister Sexy, there would be no way I could keep myself from fucking him. At some point it would happen. There was a reason I exposed myself to handsome alpha males as little as possible. I had no willpower when the time came to deny their sexual demands.

I spread my fingers apart and peeked through them. "He's a man, Kate. We can't have a man working here. I despise men. Especially men like him. You know that. What happened last time?"

"You don't want me to fire him, do you?" She gave me puppy dog eyes. "He just started this morning."

"We don't have a defined probationary period. You can't fire him without cause. We'll just wait for him to fuck up. It's only a matter of time. He's got to be out of his element."

She sighed. "I think he'll do great."

I lowered my head to the desk. "I suppose that's his Harley beside Janine's Jag?"

"It sure is."

He was a tattooed biker. Perfect. Just fucking perfect.

I closed my eyes. "Don't forget to close the door."

Within minutes, I was passed out cold. During my drunken slumber, I had a vivid dream about the new receptionist.

I'd taken him to a showing for some ridiculous reason. After the client left, Mister Sexy bent me over the kitchen island. In shock but unwilling to oppose his sexual advances, I complied with his demands. He grabbed a fistful of my hair. With one strong tug, he tore my panties and tossed them aside. Using his scuffed boots, he kicked the insides of my feet, forcing me to widen my stance. When he penetrated me, I howled like I was being branded by a red-hot poker.

He liked it rough.

His tattooed hands were everywhere. Each time he slapped my ass, the sound echoed throughout the vacant home. He squeezed my tits so firmly that I nearly reached climax. The web of one hand tightened around my throat. His stamina was remarkable. Like a jackhammer, he pounded himself into me for all eternity. Breathless, I allowed him to fulfill his every desire. In time, his breathing became irregular. His cock swelled to twice its size. My clit throbbed with each thrust that followed. On the cusp of an orgasm, I peered over my shoulder.

His head had been replaced with Margaret Seever's.

I awoke in a panic. Still drunk and somewhat confused, I stumbled to the hallway. I gazed toward the reception area. Mister Sexy's tattooed hand was cradling the phone's receiver.

A low laugh escaped him. "One moment, Janice. Let me see if she's in." He tapped his index finger against one button and then another. "Janine, I've got Janice Williams on line one . . . All right, I'll put her through."

He appeared to be doing rather well for his first day at work. No matter how good he was at his job, I eventually needed to find a reason to let him go.

If not, my dream was going to become a reality.

The last time I let that happen, it ended disastrously.

CHAPTER THREE

DEVIN

By Friday morning, I knew fuck-all about being a receptionist. But after a week of inspirational YouTube videos, instructional seminars, and reading blog posts, I felt I could at least survive.

According to the internet, there were only four rules for being a good receptionist. One, *love a ringing phone*. Two, *love your job*. Three, *leave the attitude at home*. And four, *the customer is your passion*.

I got along with anyone willing to get along with me. That made the job requirements easy, as long as I didn't have to deal with someone who was disrespectful. Being rude toward me—or the four and a half women I was hired to serve—was a different subject altogether. Convinced working with an all-woman team should be a breeze, I happily answered each phone call and hoped for the best.

With her purse over one shoulder and a leather bag over the other, Teddi came out of her office and made a beeline for the front door. I'd never considered pantsuits to be flattering until I saw her hourglass-shaped body encompassed by one. It accentuated every curve.

I clenched my jaw as she strolled past, talking on her phone. She looked to be all of five-foot-three in four-inch heels. Her curvaceous body would cause any man to embarrass himself by staring. Somewhat protected by the upper platform of my desk, I did just that, following her every move by swiveling my chair in her direction as she glided across the floor.

Just as she reached the door, she dropped her phone into her purse. She stood for a moment, staring into the parking lot. Then she turned around. She was coming straight for me. I diverted my eyes to my computer monitor and jiggled the mouse.

When she arrived, I was scrolling through available properties in Naples, trying my best to appear preoccupied— and disinterested in her.

"What's your name again?" she asked.

I looked up. The bottoms of her tits were resting against the marble countertop. Her white blouse was unbuttoned enough to reveal more than a hint of cleavage. I had to force myself not to stare.

"Oh. I didn't notice you," I said, lying through my teeth. "Sorry. It's Devin."

"Well, Devin. I'm expecting a call this morning. Kurt McEvoy. If he calls, don't put him through to voicemail. Have him call my cell."

"I sure will," I said, jotting the name onto a sticky note. "Is that all?"

She adjusted the strap of her purse, giving me an opportunity to catch another glimpse of her ample cleavage.

The instant I tore my eyes from her glorious mounds, she met my gaze with a curious look. "Do you know basic guy things?"

I had no idea what she was talking about, but I wasn't about to let her walk away. Not yet, anyway.

I gave her a reassuring look. "I suppose."

"The valet at Mercato door-dinged my SUV," she explained. "Is it possible to fix it without damaging it further? It's imperative that it looks like nothing ever happened. I'm anal about things, my vehicles included."

There was one man who was capable of fixing damaged paint without leaving a trace of his existence. He was a biker and a businessman but looked like a barroom brawler. His attitude arrived ten minutes before he did. He wouldn't have an ounce of patience for Teddi's pretentious attitude—and would likely tell her about it. I crossed my fingers, hoping he didn't disappoint me when it came time to put Teddi in her place.

"Ask for JR Nocera at Supreme Auto Collision," I said, laughing to myself as I spoke. "They're on Fourth, right off Tamiami. Tell him Bo"—I cleared my throat—"Devin sent you."

She flipped her blond hair over her shoulder and turned toward the door without as much as a "thank you." I rolled my chair to the edge of the desk and watched her walk all the way to her SUV. By the time she got into the vehicle, my dick was as stiff as stone.

Of the three women I'd been exposed to so far, two of them were completely safe. One of them wasn't. Not at all. It was going to take some serious convincing for me to keep my hands off Teddi.

The majority of my morning was spent fielding phone calls and patching them through to Janine and Kate. Convinced the job was going to become mundane, I spent my idle time watching tutorials on YouTube.

While I watched a video on how to please an angry phone caller, Kate meandered across the foyer and leaned over the edge of my desk. She beamed with pride.

"What are you so damned happy about?" I asked.

"I ate an oyster this weekend," she replied proudly. "Two, actually. Two different types, not two oysters."

I swiveled my chair to face her. "Really?"

"I tried them raw, just so I could say I did. That was interesting. About like I expected, really. I didn't like the texture. Then I decided to try them Rockefeller style."

"And you liked them?"

"They were awesome. Really rich, but they tasted great," she said. "I ate the entire order."

"I'm proud of you."

She curtsied. "Thank you."

Kate was nothing short of adorable. Bubbly, energetic, and always smiling, it was impossible not to like her. I told myself being sexual with any of the women I was working with was a bad idea. As much as I hated the idea of it, I needed to keep things platonic between Kate and me.

"What did your date think?" I asked. "When you ate them?"

She made a pouty face. "I didn't have one."

"Why not?"

Her mood shifted from almost flirty playful to being outwardly uneasy in an instant. Although I didn't intend to, I'd obviously hit a nerve.

"I'm just taking it slow," she replied. "My last relationship ended poorly. I'm going to be careful about who I go out with."

I didn't know what to say, so I said what everyone else probably did upon hearing that news. "Sorry about your last relationship."

"That's okay." She wrinkled her nose. "He was an asshole."

"Why were you with him?"

"He wasn't an asshole at first. He kind of became one over time."

The majority of men were assholes. Some had the ability to disguise the fact better than others. Once a man revealed his other-than-favorable self, I couldn't understand why a woman would remain in that type of relationship.

I asked the inevitable. "Why did you stay?"

"I think women fear being single. So we tell ourselves it isn't that bad. That it could be worse. That maybe something we did brought it on."

"You didn't make him an asshole. Believe me."

"I know that now," she said with a muted laugh. "Women are different than men. Once we're committed to someone, it's difficult to envision ourselves without them. We're convinced it wouldn't be any better with anyone else, so we put up with a lot of shit that we shouldn't. The next thing we know, we're being used, abused, taken advantage of, you name it. We just put up with it, telling ourselves that one day it'll get better."

"It didn't get better?"

She shook her head. "It got worse."

"So, you finally walked away?"

"I ran, actually."

I chuckled, trying to make light of the situation. "Couldn't get out of there fast enough, huh?"

An awkward silence followed. She gazed blankly at my computer monitor for most of it.

"He hit me," she murmured.

I tried to contain my anger but suspected she could see right through the thin veil of indifference I was hiding behind.

Still looking away, she continued in a soft, monotone

voice. "He'd pushed me a few times and he'd slapped me when we were arguing, but he'd never hit me. Then, one night, he did. With his fist—"

"Does he still live around here?" I asked, interrupting her midsentence. My inner self exploded with rage. Outwardly, I doubted I hid my anger totally. I did the best I was able.

"He... Yeah. He's got a new girlfriend, and he lives in Bonita Beach..." She paused and gave me a serious look. "Don't even think about doing anything. I'm over him. It's been six months. I'm over it." She managed a faint smile. "What about you?"

I wasn't. I never would be. I fought to contain myself. "Am I over it?"

"No." She leaned onto the edge of the elevated countertop. "I meant do you eat your oysters alone?"

"I do."

"Why?" she asked. "Are you an asshole?"

"All men are assholes."

"You don't seem like an asshole."

"I hide it well," I said. "I limit expressing my physical frustrations to men, and I vent my emotional frustrations on my bike. In the end, that leaves everyone else with a decent guy to be around."

"You're better than decent," she said.

I wasn't, but there was no value in arguing about it. I needed everyone at work to believe I was one of the good guys. Especially Kate. Still angry about the man who hit her, I forced a smile. "Thanks."

"Does riding your motorcycle really help? Does it, like, I don't know... Calm you?"

I'd had a motorcycle my entire life. Without it, I'd be a

disaster. While most men in prison yearned for a woman, a thick steak, a cup of real coffee, or their favorite fast food, I wanted nothing more than a few hundred miles of open road and a full tank of gas.

"It doesn't matter how bad things get," I replied. "There's not much a ride on that bike won't fix. A thirty-minute cruise will squash an entire day of frustrations."

She leaned away from the desk and brushed the wrinkles from her dress. "Are you really an asshole?"

"I can be."

"I think we all can be."

"I'm difficult to be with," I admitted. "Knowing that about myself prevents me from being in a relationship. Hell, it prevents me from one-night stands. I tell myself I'm an asshole to make myself feel better about being perpetually single."

"Why are you difficult to be with?"

I had the capacity to be in a relationship with the right woman. Finding that woman had proven impossible in all my years. My sexual preferences weren't in line with any women I'd ever met. I wondered if there was such a woman.

"Do you want the truth or a lie?" I asked.

Her eyes widened with wonder. She glanced over each shoulder and then leaned forward. "The truth," she whispered.

Kate was open-minded regarding my criminal history. I hoped she was equally understanding about my sexual shortcomings.

"I'm a sexual misfit," I said. "To be in a relationship, I need to be with someone open-minded. Open-minded and quite adventurous." I looked at her sideways. "*Really* open-minded. Without that person, there's no sense in me trying."

She seemed confused. "Can you define what a sexual misfit is?"

"Can I be candid?"

She slapped my bicep. "You big dork." She glanced around the foyer. "It's just you and me talking. Yes. Be candid. You're not going to offend me, if that's what you're thinking."

"Ass slapping, hair pulling, biting, shoving my cock down someone's throat. Humiliation. Saying degrading things, all of which I don't necessarily mean. Stuff like that. It's not a desire, it's a necessity."

"Oh. Wow." She blinked. Repeatedly. "That's interesting."

"Is it?"

"It is." She drifted into deep thought. "I'll see if I can find you someone," she said, meeting my gaze. "I've got an idea or two."

The thought of her finding someone was laughable. If she could, I'd entertain a relationship until I was released from the federal government's clutch.

I chuckled at the thought. "Okay."

"For clarification's sake, I'm Miss Missionary."

"By choice, or by default?"

"Choice," she replied. "I tried rough sex. Hated it. I like it slow and easy."

I wasn't disappointed to hear her sexual preferences. If anything, I was somewhat relieved. It placed her in a category that assured I wouldn't fuck up what little bit of a friendly relationship we'd developed.

"At least you know what you like," I said.

She gave me a half-assed grin and an equally unassertive nod. Then, a lightbulb appeared to go off.

"Have you ever had a girlfriend?" she asked excitedly.

"I was seeing a girl on and off before prison," I replied. "I think she got married. Why?"

"No. A girlfriend. Like, a girl, and she's your friend. She's like your guy friends, only a girl."

"I can't say that I have."

"Do you want one?"

I gave her a look. "You?"

"Uh-huh." She nodded eagerly. "I'm not gonna lie. I'm fascinated with you. We could hang out. Find new places to eat. Talk. I'd help you out with girl problems. You could help me out with guy problems. I know everyone in town. I could help you find a freaky partner. You could help me find a guy who's not an asshole." Her eyes narrowed. "No sex," she said, wagging her index finger at me as she spoke. "I mean it."

I had no one other than a cantankerous old army veteran to talk to. He was entertaining, but our conversations were all over the place. What was for dinner, *Wheel of Fortune*, who was parked in the neighbor's drive, and his bowel movements were his biggest concerns. Having access to a woman's mind beyond the walls of the office sounded like a great idea.

I nodded. "I'd love to."

"It has to be platonic," she said, still doing the finger-in-my-face thing. "No tricks."

I raised my pinkie. "Want to pinkie swear?"

Grinning from ear to ear, she hooked her pinkie to mine. "I hope you're not the type to break promises."

"Real bikers don't break promises."

"Are you the real deal?"

One of the summer's daily torrential downpours was underway. It was dumping water so rapidly, I couldn't see my motorcycle. It resembled a hurricane.

"I'll let you decide." I nodded my head toward the parking lot. "I'm riding to lunch in *that*."

She glanced at the rainstorm. She shook her head. "No,

you're not." She pulled her pinkie away and kissed it. "Friends don't let friends ride to lunch in the rain."

CHAPTER FOUR

TEDDI

It took me a week to have professional photos taken and have a graphic designer format new flyers, datasheets, and sales literature for Margaret's home. It was time to meet with everyone and advise them of our new approach.

I glanced around the conference room table. "Where is she?"

"She's on the phone," Kate replied.

"Can you remind her that we're meeting, please? She's probably talking to that idiot in Port Royal."

"Be right back," Kate said cheerily.

Port Royal, a neighborhood situated in Naples Bay, consisted of four hundred homes that ranged in price from six million to sixty million dollars. Each residence had water access through the bay's channels. None had a private beach, nor did they have a view of the gulf. One of their residents, a man in his late sixties, had shown interest in Janine—who was thirty-four years his junior—during an open house. Based solely on his wealth, she was considering hooking up with him.

Naples was a great place to be a real estate agent. With the second-highest rate of millionaires per capita in the United States, there was in excess of a billion dollars being spent on homes each year. The problem—and it was a big one for young single women—was that the average age in the city was sixty-five. Considering there were fifteen thousand registered high school students who ranged in age from fourteen to eighteen in a city that was alleged to have a population of roughly twenty thousand permanent residents, the average *realistic* age of most men in the city was eighty.

I looked at Rhea. "She hasn't fucked that guy, has she?"

"Not yet." She cringed. "Not that I know of, anyway."

Rhea was a hard worker, but she lacked experience. She'd been in my employ for a little over a year. She had a great personality, was the only one of us who was married, and she was driven to succeed by a desire to provide for her three children.

"Good work on that Crayton Road property," I said. "That wasn't on the listing long enough to be in print. Then it was gone."

"I had a buyer pocketed for it," she replied.

Low seven-figure properties were Rhea's specialty. The traffic on such homes was a constant stream of available clients, provided they were priced accordingly. The differences between selling a three-million-dollar home and a thirty-million-dollar home were vast.

In Naples, three-million-dollar homes were the norm. They were typically sold within a week of being listed, often to a buyer who hadn't even seen the property in person. The buyers for a thirty-million-dollar home were far more discriminative. They were versed on styles, finishes, types of appliances used, and location. They knew what they wanted, wouldn't settle for less, and were willing to pay more than listing price for a home that met their long list of requirements.

Kate returned with Janine in tow. As they took their

seats, I glared at Janine. "You haven't fucked that guy, have you?"

She grinned. "Not yet."

I fake-barfed. "If you do, I'll vomit."

"He's worth over two hundred million," she bragged.

"The fact that you're using that as justification makes it even more disgusting." I looked at Kate. "Evelyn is in Tampa, in training, right?"

"Until Friday."

Evelyn was a part-time intern who assisted us in our endeavors. She aspired to become a real estate agent. For me to entertain using her as one, she needed to retain a mountain of knowledge regarding construction policies, standards, and practices. Merely having a license in the Southwest Florida market wasn't enough to impress a knowledgeable buyer. One needed to be able to talk the talk and walk the walk.

I glanced around the table. It seemed empty. "I guess this is it?"

"Devin's not here," Kate said.

"Who?" I asked, although I knew perfectly well who she was speaking of.

She tilted her head toward the door. "The receptionist?"

The last thing I needed was to be drooling over the man I'd been daydreaming about. I rolled my eyes so heavily they ached. "I don't know that we need him in here. Do we?"

"Seriously?" She looked at me like I was nuts. "He's our first point of contact for new customers. Sixty percent of our buyers are first-time clients. If we're having a strategic meeting, he needs to attend."

Kate was right. She was always right. Second-in-command with the company, she was a wealth of information about Naples, the neighborhoods, the homes, and the often-fluctuating market. She retained information like a sponge held water. It didn't diminish the fact that I'd likely make a fool of myself in his presence.

"Fine. Go get him," I said with a wave of my hand. "What's his name again?"

"Devin," she said. "Devin Wallace."

I opened the file on Margaret's home. When Kate and the undeniably handsome receptionist returned, I lifted the home's datasheets from the file. Intending to pay minimal attention to the tattooed distraction, I gazed at the file as I explained my dilemma.

"The home detailed on these sheets is an exclusive listing." I blindly slid the sheets across the table. "Almost twelve thousand square feet, five bedrooms, and nine bathrooms. It's situated on Gordon Drive and has its own nearly two-hundred-foot-wide private section of sugar sand beach. The views from each bedroom—all of which face the gulf—are breathtaking. I'll admit I've been a little lackluster on getting interested clients into the property."

I let out a long sigh. I had no alternative but to lean on my team to assist me, or I was going to lose the listing.

My status in the industry would plummet.

I looked up. "To be honest," I continued, "I find this home repulsive. It's probably prevented me from investing the time and effort I should to get it sold within the conditions of the contract." I alternated glances from one person to the next. "I need to make sure this piece of property is everyone's priority for the next fifty-three days." My gaze went from Kate to the last person at the table, Mister Sexy. "If it's not sold, we're going to lose the listing."

I had every intention of looking away, but I couldn't force myself to peel my eyes off him. Other than a drunken encounter that I barely recalled, the only contact I had with him was when I passed by his desk in a rush. Now that he was sitting within arm's reach of me, I realized just how disgustingly handsome—and tattooed—he was. Wearing a powder-blue long-sleeved shirt with the sleeves rolled halfway up his tattooed forearms, he looked like he was posing for a cologne ad in a magazine.

I ogled him like he was up for auction.

The backs of his hands, entirely, were tattooed. One was covered by a lavender-colored flower and the other with a black-and-gray sugar skull. Various unidentifiable symbols covered the knuckles of each hand. The colorful tattoos continued up each forearm, disappearing beneath the cuffs of his shirt. I wondered where—and if—they stopped.

He studied the datasheet intently.

Mesmerized by his tattoos—and his honey-colored eyes—I gawked like he was a ten-car pileup of exotic cars on Highway 41.

He shifted his eyes from the folded paper to me. "They put hardwood in a Mediterranean home? Why?"

"Huh?" I muttered.

He glanced at the datasheet. "How many square feet of the home is hardwood?"

"Excuse me?"

"Hardwood," he said. "How much hardwood..."

Beyond *hardwood*, I heard nothing. My mind made the phallic connection between Margaret's flooring and what I suddenly recalled about the *hard wood* Devin was packing in his jeans on the day we met.

My pussy ached for him. I was sure everyone could see my discomfort. There was a reason I didn't employ handsome men, and this was it.

I crossed my legs. "What does it matter?"

"Short of someone who wants a Mediterranean home with the warmth of a cave, no one is going to move into this home," he explained. "If they can't see themselves in it, convincing them to buy it is going to be impossible. It would be cost prohibitive to change the architecture, and it would be a nightmare to re-trim the place with lighter wood, but the flooring could be redone with something brighter and more inviting. That alone would change a potential buyer's perception entirely."

His ability to communicate astounded me. Nevertheless, he was out of his mind. The change would cost half a million dollars or more. "I can't change the flooring. It would cost half a mil—"

"What would you lose in commission if this listing was pulled?"

The last time I revealed my income to a man, it ended disastrously. I mentally cocked my hip and peered down my nose at him. "I don't think that's any of your business."

"No?" His look hardened. "Do you want my help or not?"

"I want ideas and action on selling this property," I snapped back. "I don't need some tattooed biker who has no knowledge of—"

He shot a *fuck you* glare right at me.

He stood and leaned toward the center of the table. "If I didn't have knowledge, I'd be listening, not speaking. I've worked here for eight days. I don't expect you to respect me. Hell, you haven't spoken to me more than twice in passing.

But if you want me to be a member of this team, you'll treat me in a respectful manner. If you don't, or if you ever talk to me in that disrespectful tone again, I'll walk out of here so fast it'll make your head spin."

My heart was in my throat. Incapable of speaking, I simply stared back at him like a mindless idiot.

"Obviously you didn't review my application," he said, still looming over me. He crossed his arms over his wide chest. "If you had, you'd know a few things about me. Because you didn't and you don't, I'll hit the highlights. I was born and raised here. I have nearly fifteen years of construction experience. Ten of them were spent overseeing the construction of homes that would make this ugly son of a bitch look like an Italian cracker box. Based on my experience, I'd suggest spending a little less than a hundred grand on flooring. It would make the home appeal to a wider market, and it would only cut your commission by a few percent. If you're too stubborn, too money hungry, or just too goddamned blind to see the benefit in making that change, leave it the way it is." He tossed the datasheet in front of me. "I'm sure you'll sit on it for another hundred and eighty days."

He was Alpha with a capital A.

To minimize my discomfort from my wet panties, I wagged my knees back and forth and hoped he couldn't sense my state of arousal.

I gave him an apologetic look. "You're telling me that I can get that floor done for less than a hundred grand?"

"Between fifty-five and ninety, depending on what you want to put in place of what's there. It won't be the quality of the rest of the home's interior finishes, but it'll get the home sold, and that's what matters."

I sold homes. I didn't build them. I had no idea what real-world construction costs were. When I'd asked for previous clients, the prices I'd been given were ten times what he was suggesting.

"Are you sure?" I asked.

He arched an argumentative eyebrow.

I swallowed a lump of humility. "Can you get me an exact quote?"

"I can get you a damned good one," he replied. "As long as you're not opposed to having a few *tattooed bikers* in there doing the work. Before you ask and piss me off even more, yes, they're licensed."

Feeling defeated—and horny as hell—I glanced around the room. Three wide-eyed women and one stern-looking man were staring back at me.

"Does anyone else have something to add?" I asked.

The meek silence that followed was deafening. If no one had anything constructive to say, I desperately needed to change my panties. I closed the folder.

"Meeting adjourned," I squeaked.

CHAPTER FIVE

DEVIN

Herb Riley was a family friend. Following my father's death, he and I became rather close. He insisted at the time of my incarceration that I list his home as my residence. Unlike state prison, federal prison requires approval of an inmate's proposed residence prior to them being released. If the residence is preapproved, the transition from incarceration to freedom is seamless.

A former brigadier general in the US Army and a decorated combat veteran, Herb wore his gray hair in a crew cut, woke every morning at four thirty, and briskly walked the neighborhood's four-mile footpath prior to breakfast each day. He was opinionated, argumentative, and entertaining. One thing he wasn't?

Delicate.

"First she talks to you like you're some punk kid," Herb said. "Then she spends the next week and a half parading by your desk in tight dresses while giving you the stink eye?"

"Pretty much," I replied. "I keep waiting for her to apologize, but she hasn't. Not yet, at least."

"If she treated me like that, I'd have told that bitch to go fuck a goat."

"Just dive right into a bestiality conversation right there

in the meeting?" I chuckled at the thought. "In front of all those other women? That would have gotten me some points for originality, I suppose."

He gave me a contemptuous look. "I was being facetious."

I raised my cup in a toast. "I was being a smartass."

"Comes natural, doesn't it?"

"More or less."

"Your dad was a smartass," he said, laughing as if recalling my father's lack of a filter. "Mouth got him in trouble on numerous occasions. Son of a bitch had a temper, too. When he built that house for me on the south end of town, he punched the stonemason right in the cocksucker. Dropped him like a sack of shit, right there in the kitchen."

Following a long bout with breast cancer, my mother passed away when I was in high school. My father died of a heart attack fourteen years later, nearly three years before I went to prison. Losing him caused a downward spiral of my emotions. My life soon followed. Hoping to save myself from complete destruction, I joined a motorcycle club.

Being in the club gave me a sense of belonging. The men I rode with were the siblings I never had. The MC soon became my family—one I was prohibited from returning to until my federally mandated supervised release was over.

"My father's high blood pressure cost him his life," I said. "I'm trying to keep my temper at bay."

His wiry brows pinched together. "Biting your lower lip doesn't change your DNA. You are who you are."

He was right. Despite my desire to refrain from losing my temper, it seemed to eventually rear its ugly head. I'd used sex as an outlet in the past, but my options in that respect were currently nonexistent.

I carried my plate to the sink. "While we're on that subject, do you know any of the other girls who work for Teddi?"

"Are we done talking about that inconsiderate bitch you're working for?"

I rinsed my plate and put it in the dishwasher before turning to face him. "For now, I suppose."

"You want to know if I know one of those gals?"

"Katelyn Winslow. She's one of the agents. She goes by Kate."

He glanced over his shoulder. "Winslow?"

I nodded. "Yep."

He lowered his gaze. He rubbed the backs of his sun-spotted hands. "Can't say I do. Why?"

"The guy she was seeing punched her in the face. Guess he lives here in—"

He spun around. "He did what?"

I didn't like it any more than he did. "You heard me," I said, taking my seat. "He smacked her in the face."

"Sounds like there's someone besides your employer who needs to be taught a lesson on the difference between right and wrong. If I find that cocksucker, I tell you what. I'll butt-fuck him."

"You're out of your mind, old man."

He glared. "According to who?"

"Me." I shook my head in disbelief. "You're going to fuck a guy in the butt?"

"Sounds like that prick needs it."

"While you're talking about sticking your cock in a guy's poop shoot, your wife's turning over in her grave."

"Butt-fucking isn't sexual," he argued. "You do it because you're angry at the recipient, not because you're attracted to them."

When Teddi snapped at me during the meeting, I wanted to bend her over the table and fuck her like she owed me money. Since then, I'd thought about it on numerous occasions for no other reason than to teach her a lesson about how she treated me.

I laughed, partially at Herb's remarks and a little at the thought of butt-fucking Teddi. I'd get tremendous satisfaction out of it, but there was no way it would ever happen. She was far too uppity to offer herself to a tattooed biker.

It didn't mean I couldn't throw a bottle of wine in my saddlebag and give it to her as a peace offering. From what I knew of her, a little alcohol would certainly loosen her up. What happened afterward would be anyone's guess.

"Enough of the butt talk," I said. "I was just thinking I'd pay that guy a visit if could find out who he was."

He rose from his seat and riffled through a drawer. After producing a pen and notepad, he scribbled something down. "How the fuck is Katelyn spelled?"

"Hers is K-A-T-E-L-Y-N."

"That's what I figured." He finished writing and pushed the small pad to the side. "I'll find the prick. Don't worry."

"You're a detective now?"

He peered into his coffee cup and then looked at me like something was terribly wrong. "When did I pour this?"

"About the time I took my toast out of the toaster."

A confused look washed over him. "You drink any of it when I was taking a shit?"

"I was scrambling eggs when you took a shit."

"Just thought I'd ask." He looked at me with concern in his eyes. "Seems like it either evaporated or someone stole it."

"Why would I drink your coffee when I have my own?"

"That's the same question I'm sitting here asking myself,"

he replied. "All I can come up with is that you're an ornery fucker."

"No, Herb," I said. "I didn't drink your coffee."

"Back to the asshole who hit the girl." He stood and walked to the coffeepot. "I might not be a detective, but I'm resourceful. You ever heard of the six degrees of separation?" He glanced over his shoulder. "I'm only six handshakes away from knowing that crazy bastard in North Korea, the redheaded girl with the nice tits, and that prick who hit the girl. Mark my words, I'll find him."

"When you do, let me know."

"I might and I might not." He sipped his fresh coffee. "I'll ask Vinnie when I see him at the clubhouse this afternoon. He's got more money than sense. I bet he knows how to find that prick."

The *redheaded girl* comment registered. I couldn't care less about Herb's card-playing friends. I wondered if there was someone in the neighborhood I needed to meet. "Who's the redheaded girl with nice tits?"

"Johansson, or whatever her name is. She's in those movies with Tony Stark. She wears that tight suit, and the damned thing fits her like a glove. Looks like she's trying to smuggle a couple of cantaloupes out of the farmer's market over on Pine Ridge. I wouldn't butt-fuck her, I'd poke it right between her big fat knockers."

I shook my head. "Like I said, if you find him—"

"I heard you the first time," he grumbled. "I might be old, but I'm not deaf. Or stupid."

I glanced at my watch. If I stopped talking and left, there would be time to go by the liquor store before work.

"I better get to work," I said. "Getting flooring quotes today."

After taking his seat, he traced his finger over Kate's name on the sheet of paper. "Better be careful talking to those old running mates of yours. If that little prick who oversees your every move finds out you're hanging around them again, you'll be back in the pokey."

"I'm not going to hang around with them," I explained. "I'm going to have them do some work for me. If they're priced right, that is."

"Damned shame your father's partner sold the company. You could have gotten those mustachioed villains who worked for him to do it for next to nothing."

My father co-owned a local construction company until his death. Although he had nothing more than a minority stake in the business, it had been a somewhat profitable venture for him. The rewards for his hard work were then squandered on my legal defense. What money he hadn't placed in a retirement account was used to fight for what I believed was right. After my conviction and subsequent sentencing, I sold his home and used the proceeds to finance the appeal of my case. When the legal smoke cleared, I'd lost much more than my freedom.

When I left prison, my motorcycle, the clothes on my back, and a mind filled with memories were my only possessions. Having previously relied on my father's company for employment, I felt starting from scratch would provide me with a sense of accomplishment. Now, win or lose, I had no one to blame but myself.

"I'm headed out." I carried my cup to the sink. "If you find anything out about that guy, let me know."

He raised his cup. "Will do."

When I was almost to the door, he cleared his throat. "Hey, dipshit. What's for dinner?"

I paused and gave it a moment's thought. Grudge-fucking Teddi seemed like a great idea, if I could pull it off.

"Go to the clubhouse." I smirked. "There's a good chance I might be late."

CHAPTER SIX

The workday was nearly over. I'd spent most of it watching Devin talk on the phone and trying to catch glimpses of him each time he walked to the bathroom. What time wasn't spent drooling over his bravado gait was spent daydreaming of what I wanted him to do to me.

I regretted not apologizing to him for the way I acted. Doing it now would require talking to him face-to-face. Talking to him made me nervous. Avoidance was the only way for me to maintain any level of sanity.

The sound of fingers snapping brought me out of my semiconscious state. I blinked my eyes into focus.

Kate was leaning against my office door. "Wake up," she said. "It's almost time to go."

"I'm awake. I was just thinking. When did you get back?"

"Just now."

"How'd it go?"

"I sent you a text." She took a few steps toward me. "Got the listing. Seven point two."

"Congratulations," I said. "That's a nice home."

"Thank you." She gave me a funny look. "What were you thinking about?"

"Oh, nothing. Why?"

She gestured toward my face with her finger. "You've kind of got a little slobbery thing going on. You might want to wipe it off."

Embarrassed, I wiped my mouth with the back of my hand. "I was just daydreaming."

"About Devin?"

"What?" I gasped. "Seriously? No."

Grinning, she gave me a look of opposition. "Are you sure?"

She'd been gone in meetings all day and had no idea of the mental turmoil I'd faced. Even so, I wasn't about to admit I'd spent the majority of my day hoping he'd get up and walk around the office. I needed to pull it together. Swimming in self-pity about Margaret's home and using Devin as my mental means of resolve wasn't healthy.

I cleared my mind of lingering thoughts and gave her an innocent look. "Why would you say something like that?"

"I see how you look at him."

"When?"

"Always."

"What does that mean?"

"It means I can see the way you look at him."

I was looking at him like any sex-starved woman would look at a hardened biker who had a cock the size of a can of Pringles. I'd deny it until I either believed it or until Kate called me out on it enough.

"I look at him like I'm scared for my life," I insisted. "Did you see how he looked at me in that meeting the other day? He was glaring at me like he wanted to carve out my heart and eat it."

She scowled. "He was not."

"How do you know?" I asked. "You were on his side of the table. You couldn't see his face."

She looked at me the same way my mother had when she knew I was lying. I tried to muster a serious look but doubted I accomplished much.

"I could see you," she said. "And your face said it all."

"I didn't look scared?"

"No, you didn't look scared." She sat down across from me and laughed. "You looked hopeful. The last time I saw you look at someone like that was when . . . You know when it was."

"Don't mention his name," I said. "I mean it."

"I won't. But"—she raised her brows and lowered her chin—"you looked at him the same way you looked at Devin."

I was afraid of that. I needed to find a way to conceal my feelings, or I was going to end up in trouble. If I was wearing my sexual thoughts like a jeweled crown, the women I worked with wouldn't be the only ones who'd be able to see it. It would only be a matter of time until Mister Sexy could peer right through my translucent mask.

"I did not," I insisted. I situated a few things on my desk. The distraction did little to rid my mind of sexual thoughts. It had been way too long since I'd been in a real man's presence. Dumbfounded as to why I had a stuffed pink starfish on my desk, I raised it in wonder. "Do you know where this came from?"

"Stop changing the subject."

I tossed it into the trash. "Other than the meeting, I really haven't spoken to him. You two seem to talk a lot. What's he like?"

"He's nice. He's respectful." She picked some lint from her blouse. "His dad used to own a construction company in town. That's where he got his experience. He lives with that old man, Herb." She looked up. "I guess he was friends with Devin's dad."

"He makes me nervous," I said. "Not Herb. Devin."

Her eyes narrowed. "Why?"

I wished I hadn't mentioned it. The only thing that made me nervous was that I knew I had zero ability to resist Devin if he made any sexual advances toward me. Rugged alpha males, homemade cookies, and sweet wine were my weaknesses. Only one of them would cause my life to spiral downward until I hit rock bottom.

"I don't know," I said. "I think it's just the way he looks at me. It's like I'm made of glass."

"Listen to this." She leaned onto the front edge of my desk. "Devin and I went to lunch at that new hamburger place in Mercato the other day, and Paul Trevotti came in. He was wearing flip-flops, a pair of faded shorts, and a crappy Rolling Stones concert tee. Devin watched him sit down and said, 'See that guy. He's got money. Serious money.' I asked how he knew. He said, 'I can just tell by how he walks.' Maybe he learned how to read people when he was...umm..." She wrung her hands together.

"When he was what?" I asked. "You can't just stop like that, Kate. You always do that."

"When he was in the motorcycle club."

Visions of Jax Teller from the *Sons of Anarchy* came to mind. My entire body began to tingle. I swallowed against a lump of desire as it slowly rose in my throat.

"He was in a motorcycle club?" I murmured.

"He was." She began picking at her blouse again. "He's not now."

It was time we change the subject. If not, Kate would continue discussing Devin just to watch me squirm. She was a wonderful person—and my best friend—but she derived tremendous pleasure by living vicariously through others. It wasn't uncommon for her to suggest men—who she would never personally date—to clients, coworkers, and friends. She would then press them for information about their relationship, leaving nothing off-limits.

She was far too sensible to venture away from her vanilla lifestyle. Having others do it was as close as she'd ever get. I wasn't interested in becoming one of her guinea pigs. If we continued discussing Devin, I'd be a complete wreck. I simply needed to avoid him until I built up a hatred toward his mere existence. It would come in time. It always did, eventually.

"Enough about him," I said, mentally shaking my head to clear it of impure thoughts. "What else is going on?"

Her eyes danced around my office playfully while she thought of something to say. She lifted a blown-glass paperweight off my desk and studied it. "Do you know anyone who is single and leans toward the freaky side of sex?"

My eyes bulged. "What?"

She set the sphere down and glared. "Shhh." She glanced toward the door. "Your door is open."

"You're the one asking questions about freaky sex," I whispered. "What are you talking about?"

"This conversation is between you and me," she said. "You're not going to use it against anyone. Promise?"

I sighed. "I'm not a child."

She gave me a side-eyed look. "Promise?"

"Okay," I whined. "I promise."

Her mouth twisted into a guilty grin. "Now I'm not sure if

I should say anything."

"You can't ask a question like that and then not elaborate," I said. "Spill it."

She sighed. "Devin likes rough sex. Really rough sex. He said it's all but impossible to find someone who can . . ."

My ears began to ring, drowning out everything she said after *rough sex*. Kate knew me well enough to know I was the type of woman she was asking about. She also realized I wasn't interested in a relationship. I hoped she knew I wasn't willing to fuck an employee. Especially after the last catastrophe.

"What are you doing?" I asked.

Still babbling about Devin's sexual preferences, she paused. "Huh?"

"I'm not interested in him," I said. "If that's what you're trying to—"

"Oh. Not at all," she said, shaking her head. Her mouth curled into a mischievous grin. "I'm just asking for a friend."

"Kate . . ."

She raised her hands in surrender. "I'm serious."

I tapped a pen against the edge of my desk. "He's sexy. He's a freak. He's handsome. He's alpha as hell. He's handsome. He's also exactly what I don't need in my life. I'm not interested. I can't take that chance. Not again."

"You said *handsome* twice."

"No I didn't."

"You did," she insisted. "Twice."

"Whatever."

"Well, I wasn't suggesting you consider him. I was just . . . Anyway." She shrugged as if it was no big deal. "If you think of anyone, let me know."

I studied her. It was impossible to tell if she was trying

to help Mister Sexy or if she was trying to plant a seed in my mind. She was always smiling, which made reading her moods difficult to say the least.

"Yeah. I'll ask around town," I said in a sarcastic tone.

A knock on my door startled the hell out of me. I darted my eyes to the doorway.

Standing in the center of the opening with his arms crossed, Devin was looking right at me. "Couple of the fellas want to meet at the property and have a look at it." He glanced at his watch. "You want to ride on the back of my bike or take your broom?"

My gaze fell to the desk. "If I haven't said I was sorry, I am."

"You didn't. I appreciate it." He took a few steps toward me. "To keep from pissing off the population on Gordon Drive, I should probably ride with you, though. My bike's liable to wake everyone up from their afternoon naps. They might hold you responsible."

He was right about the neighborhood's perception of a Harley with loud pipes. Riding with me wasn't an option, though.

"When do they want to meet?" I asked.

"Thirty minutes."

If he got in the car with me, his raised handprints would be on my ass cheeks before the night was over. I needed a way out, and I needed it fast.

"Ride with Kate," I said. "I'll meet you two there."

"No can do," Kate said, tapping her index finger against the face of her watch. "I'm meeting someone for drinks."

"When?" I blurted.

"Thirty minutes." She stood. "Twenty, really."

"Where's Janine?"

"Estero."

I looked at Devin. Remembering the mistakes of my past was crucial to my success. If being hornswoggled out of my savings, cheated on, and humiliated wasn't enough, nothing would be.

I reached for my purse. "Give me two minutes. I'll meet you at the door."

He undressed me with his eyes. "All right."

My gaze fell to his crotch.

His burrito twitched.

Fearing I was losing my mind, I met his gaze. I needed reassurance that what I thought happened hadn't.

He winked and turned away.

I quickly looked to Kate's chair. It was empty.

I drew a breath of courage and headed for the door. If we didn't stop for drinks, everything should be fine.

Just fine.

CHAPTER SEVEN

DEVIN

Sitting within a few feet of Teddi in her Range Rover, it was impossible to deny her natural beauty. In a city where Botox injections, breast enhancements, and liposuction were the norm, she appeared to be sans any visible enhancements.

Although I hated to admit it, there was really no room for Teddi to improve in the looks department. Personality-wise, however, she could've used an augmentation. She hadn't said two words since we left the office.

To keep myself from nursing a stiff dick for the entire ride, I attempted to gaze straight ahead during most of the trip across town. When the occasion arose, I stole quick glances at her. Any man deprived of sexual contact for eight years would have done the same thing.

Her blond hair was pinned in a bun. The skintight tangerine dress she wore had a low neckline and thin straps that draped over each shoulder. Her right wrist was decorated with multiple gold bracelets and her left with a gold watch. Two gold necklaces dangled over a valley of cleavage that garnered my attention each time I looked in her direction.

As much as I hoped to stare straight at the road ahead, my eyes rattled back and forth like a pachinko ball.

Teddi complained about an elderly driver in a Bentley

convertible. I took the opportunity to take another look at her gravity-defying tits.

"I can't believe she's just sitting there," Teddi seethed. "The light's been green for at least sixty seconds."

"I can't believe you haven't honked."

"It doesn't matter how mad I get, I don't honk. I hate it when people do that to me, so I don't do it to them."

I made note that she was a compassionate driver. It did little to dissolve the frustration that remained from how disrespectful she'd been in the meeting. While she gripped the steering wheel with such force that it turned her knuckles white, I took another look at her magnificent tits.

Traffic cleared just as the signal changed from green to yellow. Teddi turned the steering wheel to the right and punched the gas. My road bag slid from my lap, revealing my current state of arousal. As I fumbled to slide the leather satchel back into place, Teddi glanced in my direction.

Not wanting her to think I was interested in her sexually, I slid the worn leather bag over my rigid dick.

I looked at her like she'd purposefully backed over my motorcycle in the parking lot. "You should warn a guy before you do something like that."

"What's in that bag, anyway?"

"Just a few things we might need."

"Tools?"

"More or less."

She gave the bag a quick look and then shifted her eyes to the road. Ten minutes of silence followed, which had been the norm for most of the trip. I wondered if she was reserved or if her dislike for tattooed bikers was something I should truly be concerned with.

We pulled into the home's gated drive and rolled to a stop. Teddi programmed the code into the keypad and waited for the gate to open. "Where are your friends?"

"I'm sure they'll be here soon."

She proceeded up the long drive, seeming slightly uneasy about something.

"What's with the apprehension?" I asked.

"Apprehension?" she stammered. "I'm not apprehensive."

"You seem like it."

"Well, I'm not," she snapped back. She parked in front of the guesthouse and left the vehicle running. "I guess we'll just wait for them to get here."

"Can we go inside and look around?" I asked.

She looked at me like I'd asked her to behead a goat. "What?"

"Inside," I said, gesturing toward the home. "Can we go inside?"

She swallowed heavily. "Do we need to?"

The driving force was apparent. She didn't want to be alone with me. Realizing it fueled me to press the issue even harder. I opened the car door and stepped outside.

"C'mon," I said, shouldering my bag. "Let's look this place over."

She got out of the car and tugged the wrinkles from her slinky dress. "Follow me," she said over the car's hood. "I'll give you a quick tour."

She conquered a pair of four-inch heels with an elegance I'd never witnessed. Each calculated step was placed perfectly in front of the other, almost as if she were walking a tightrope.

Following a ten-second-long session of being captivated by her purposeful stride, my gaze shifted to her magnificent ass. It was as wonderful as her tits. Small but more than ample for her petite frame, it complemented her small waist. Hypnotized by the rhythmic rise and fall of both ass cheeks, I watched her strut across the handlaid brick drive until she reached the door. Even though I detested her abrasive attitude, she made me hornier than a three-dicked rabbit.

She unlocked the door and stepped inside. "Well, here it is," she said with a wave of her hand. "In all its Mediterranean glory."

I stepped around her, hoping the home's unsightly interior would diffuse my state of arousal. A trace of her perfume tickled my nostrils as I walked past. She smelled better than she looked, and her looks would warrant being arrested in a handful of Middle Eastern countries. Barring an intervention, things were going to take a sexual turn. That much I was sure of.

I brushed past her. "I'll be right back," I said over my shoulder.

"Where are you going?"

"To the kitchen," I replied. "Keep an eye out for them. I'll be right back."

The home was just as hideous as the pictures depicted. High Venetian plaster ceilings, dark woods, darker tile, and a hideously out-of-place dark wood floor—it was about as welcoming as the federal prison's special housing unit or *hole*.

I laid my bag on the kitchen island and placed the bottle of wine I'd purchased in the refrigerator. After a quick survey of the flooring and trim, I was convinced the new floor would be a breeze.

Pleased with my findings, and even more thrilled with what the night might hold, I sauntered to the grand entrance.

"Any sign of them?" I asked.

She shook her head. "No."

Leaning against the door with her hands behind her back, she seemed scared to come inside.

"I took a look at the flooring in there," I said. "This is going to be a breeze."

"Do you think so?"

I unbuttoned my shirt and started to take it off.

Her eyes shot wide. "What are you doing?"

"Taking off my shirt. I don't want to get anything on it," I said, pulling it over my shoulders. "This shithole's been sitting vacant for six months. There's a layer of dust two inches thick on everything. I was going to show you something. Settle down."

She looked me up and down. "Show me *what*?"

"The flooring and trim."

I took off my shirt and folded it. Standing in front of her in a ribbed tank top, I had her undivided attention.

I extended my hand. "Here, take this."

She lifted my shirt as if it were an active bomb.

I got on my knees in front of the long stretch of baseboard that ran the length of the stairs. "Just find somewhere to put it, I guess."

Clearly flustered, she draped the shirt over a section of handrail at the bottom of the stairway. Standing at the base of the steps thirty feet to my right, she crossed her arms. "Okay. What are you going to show me?"

"Come here," I said with a laugh. "You can't see it from over there."

Her dress had worked its way to mid-thigh. As she strode across the floor in her heels, I fixed my eyes on the hem of her dress. Her thighs had compact, firm muscles, like that of a ballerina. I diverted my attention from her to the wood trim on my left.

On my hands and knees, I reached for the baseboard. "See this?" I asked, tracing my finger along the bottom of the board. "Someone's already replaced this flooring once. This wood is thinner than what was in here before. The gap between the bottom of the trim and the floor's surface is about three-sixteenths of an inch or more."

I glanced to my right. Two cream-colored Jimmy Choo's were within inches of my face. I looked up. Despite her five-foot-two height, her shapely legs stretched for a mile.

She was bent over slightly and had her eyes fixed on the baseboard. Her position and her wide-legged stance weren't by accident. The sexy little bitch was standing over me with her legs spread three feet apart.

Eight sexless years in prison took its toll like someone flipped a switch.

I stood in the twelve inches of unoccupied space between her and the wall. My chest brushed against hers as I rose.

"What the fuck are you doing?" I asked.

"I was … I was looking at the …" She nodded toward the floor. "The trim."

Our faces were so close, I could taste the spearmint on her breath. With our lips nearly touching, I looked her dead in the eye. "Unless you want me looking up your dress, you need to take a step back."

She swallowed heavily. "I should?"

"That depends." I narrowed my gaze. "Do you want me looking up your dress?"

"I'm not … I don't," she stammered. "I don't know."

After what I'd been through, I wasn't going to do anything without her expressed approval. Once she gave it, I planned to rid myself of every ounce of pent-up frustration that I harbored. When I was done, she'd know what it felt like to be grudge-fucked by a two-hundred-and-twenty-pound biker who just finished an eight-year bit in the joint.

"Well." I brushed my rigid cock against her thigh. "That's something you're going to need to decide. I can't do it for you."

The doorbell rang.

Clearly flustered—and maybe a little relieved—she quickly stepped away. After brushing the wrinkles from her dress, she fanned her face with her hand. Flushed to a deep color of red, she looked like she'd just completed a marathon.

I was hard as a rock and sexually frustrated. Looking at the flooring with two men I hadn't seen in eight years was about as shallow of a desire as I'd ever possessed. I limped to the door and grabbed the handle.

"Wait!" she said.

I glanced over my shoulder. Still fanning her face, she looked back at me innocently. If she was nothing else, she was a cute little bitch.

I raised my brows. "Well?"

She lowered her hand and nodded. "I'm ready."

"For me to open the door, or for me to look up your dress?"

"Both," she replied.

CHAPTER EIGHT

TEDDI

I was perceived as being a shrewd businesswoman. Acting that part was a lie. Playing it to the best of my ability was the only way I could survive in the real estate market. In reality, I was still the little girl who loved being led by the hand, told what to do, and complimented when I met the expectations of those giving the instructions.

In the presence of a man like Devin, I was incapable of acting with any degree of accuracy. I knew he could see through my facade. Being anyone other than my true self was the same as being caught in a lie and continuing to spin the unbelievable yarn, knowing all those within earshot realized it was nothing but a fabrication.

I was done telling the lie.

To him at least.

I fidgeted to make myself comfortable. I hoped I didn't look like I just had finished having an earth-shattering orgasm. I hadn't, but I came close when Devin brushed his chest against mine. I tidied my dress and tried to clear my head of the clutter. My panties were soaked, and my mind was mush.

Devin reached for the door. The muscles in his arm flared. I could tell he was in shape, but I'd had no idea to what degree—until he took his shirt off. The stark white wifebeater he wore clung to his flat stomach and broad chest like a coat of white paint. I tried not to stare, but I found his tattoos intriguing. His bare arms were covered with various pieces of colorful work. I darted my eyes from one to the other. As the door swung open, I knew one thing for absolute certain.

I was in over my head.

Two men, both built like lumberjacks, stood just outside the doorway. Dressed fractionally better than what I expected, they were wearing matching outfits of jeans, boots, and khaki-colored, long-sleeved shirts. A newer model Ford pickup truck was parked in the driveway behind them.

The bigger of the two men—a massive man with hands the size of Christmas hams—stepped toward Devin. His mouth twisted into a smirk. "What's shaking, Bone?"

Devin shook his hand as if he hadn't seen him for years. They embraced in a hug, each slapping the other on the back.

"Just trying to get this house sold," Devin said. "How's things on the other side of the alley?"

"Things are good, brother. Things are good," the man replied. "Damned good to see you."

"Good to be seen." Devin gestured to me. "This is Teddi. Teddi, this is—"

"Frank," the man said, gesturing to an oval-shaped patch that was sewn to the chest of his shirt. He stepped around Devin. His dark, shoulder-length hair dangled in front of his eyes, and his face was covered in a few days of stubble. He offered his hand. "Nice to meet you."

His hand engulfed mine completely. I felt small and incapable. I glanced at Devin. He gave a smile of reassurance.

I shook his hand. "Nice to meet you, Frank."

Frank released my hand and gestured over his shoulder with his thumb. "That's Shane."

Shane wasn't as tall as Frank, but he was big by any means of comparison. With his mouth curled into a permanent grin and his hair cut short, he was much less intimidating than his business partner.

I shook his hand. "Nice to meet you."

Devin clapped his hands together. "Sorry, fellas, but Teddi and I have a meeting we need to get to in about thirty minutes. We're going to need to make this quick."

Five minutes prior, I was barely capable of carrying on a meaningful conversation. Devin's declaration of our "meeting" caused me to slip right back into my mush-minded state. As my mind reeled to come up with the possibilities of what might happen between us, the men began to discuss the flooring.

"Meeting at five thirty?" Frank asked. "Other'n our dumb asses, who meets this late in the day?"

Devin gave him a nod of reassurance. "The real estate market never sleeps, does it, Teddi?"

I was in the midst of deciding if having sex with Devin was a good idea, a great idea, or a bad idea. I was nowhere near a concrete conclusion.

I shook my head to free it of the clutter. "Huh?"

Devin glared. "The real estate market never sleeps. *Does it, Teddi?*"

"Umm. No," I replied "Never."

Devin gestured to the baseboard at his feet. "This was tile at one time, and someone put this engineered wood in its place. They removed the tile when they did. This flooring is a quarter of an inch thinner than the original tile. I'm wondering if you could lay an LVT over it that looks like stone. Something to brighten it up in here."

Frank gazed at the length of the entrance and then peered into the great room. "Place looks like a dungeon."

"That's why you're here, brother."

Shane wandered down the hallway and ventured into the living area.

Frank put his hands on his hips and surveyed everything within eyeshot from floor to ceiling. "What's the square footage?"

"Almost twelve thousand," Devin replied.

"Including the guesthouse," I added.

"Used LVT on a new construction in Miami last week," Frank said. "Looked like tumbled travertine tile. When the job was almost done, the owner came in. She looked around and started screaming, 'What the hell have you done?' She thought we'd put real travertine in. Said she couldn't afford it."

In the middle of trying to figure out what one of Devin's tattoos was, I shifted my attention to Frank. "What was the installed cost?"

"We used a high-end product on that one," Frank said. "It wasn't cheap."

I'd had a feeling Devin was mistaken with his figures. I prepared myself for a letdown.

"What's *not cheap*?" I asked.

"Ten bucks a foot," Frank responded.

Ten dollars a square foot sounded reasonable to me. "That sounds like a pretty good—"

"Go to hell," Devin snarled. "I'm not giving you ten bucks a foot."

Frank shot Devin a glare. "Settle down, Bone. That's

what it cost *her*. Your girl will only have to pay about six fifty."

Your girl?

I wondered what Devin had told him about me. Maybe calling me Devin's girl was some kind of biker lingo. Either way, I liked hearing it.

"Five fifty sounds better," Devin said.

Frank's eyes thinned. "Price needs to be higher than five fifty. There's installation labor, and the tile cost four twenty-five. I tell you what, though. It looks as good as forty-five-dollar tile. Can't tell the difference."

Devin shrugged. "Five fifty sounds about right, then."

"I'm six fifty. You're five fifty," Frank said. "I'll talk to Shane and see if he's willing to meet somewhere in the middle."

Devin looked him up and down. "Didn't realize you needed permission to make a deal."

Clearly taking exception to the remark, Frank folded his arms over his massive chest. "I don't."

"I'll offer you six dollars a foot for the installed square footage," Devin said. "Loose-fit, not glued. If we put a floating floor in, the new owner can change it later if they want to. Accept it, or I'll get someone local to do it."

"Got to drive from Miami every day," Frank complained. "Two hours each way, with traffic."

"You going to wear a skirt when you do this job?" Devin asked, his voice laced with sarcasm. "You're whining like a bitch."

"God damn, Bone. At six dollars, I'm barely breaking even."

"No, you're not," Devin argued. "You're taking the first step at building a long-lasting relationship. You can't put a price on that."

"With who?" Frank asked. "Your girl, here? Miss Teddi? She gonna call me to do work when you're long gone?"

"I'll be here until my supervised release is over," Devin replied. "That's eighteen months, at least. Maybe two years. Do it for six bucks a foot or kick rocks."

Frank looked up and down the hallway and then met Devin's gaze. "Fine," he said. "I'll do it for six bucks."

Devin looked at me. "I'm guessing we're at about eight thousand square feet after we eliminate closets, bathrooms, and the guesthouse. That's just an educated guess. If it's right, we're talking forty-eight thousand. Is that a problem?"

Forty-eight thousand dollars was pocket change compared to the two-point-four million I was going to make in commission if the home sold.

"I'd like to see the product," I said.

"Shane!" Frank bellowed. "Hustle your ass out to the truck and grab some of that travertine-looking shit, would ya?"

Shane emerged from behind us. He silently sauntered past and then reappeared with a box of tile. Apparently there was a hierarchy in the motorcycle club. Devin must have been above Frank, who was clearly above Shane.

He handed the box to Frank. Frank knelt, spread eight pieces of tile on the floor, and fitted them together. He stood and stepped away.

"What's that look like?" he asked.

I studied it. It looked like stone. "It looks like travertine."

He tapped it with the toe of his boot. "Step on it."

I did as he asked. It looked—and felt—like a much more expensive travertine tile. In fact, I couldn't tell it apart. The best part was that they were going to be able to lay it over the existing flooring.

I'd spoken to Margaret about the changes I was considering. She promptly advised me to do whatever was necessary to sell the home. I didn't know if this was the right thing or not, but I needed to do something to make the home more marketable.

"Let's do it," I said. "I'll let you and Devin decide the actual square footage and final price."

"I'll have Shane grab a tape measure out of the truck," Frank said. "We can measure it up really—"

"We don't have time tonight," I said. "We're just about late for that meeting."

Frank glanced at Devin and then at me. He looked me over good. I felt like he, too, could see right through me. It must have been a biker thing.

"Shane and I need to beat feet, too," Frank said. "Shane's got a tryout with the Miami Dolphins in a few minutes. Hell, I damned near forgot."

"The Dolphins?" I asked. "Really?"

Devin looked at me like I was nuts. "He was joking."

Frank laughed and then gestured toward me. "She cool?"

Devin nodded. "She's good."

Frank looked right at me. His mouth was twisted into a smirk. "Pretty obvious the only meeting you two are having is a meeting of your uglies."

"Our uglies?"

"Yeah," he said with a nod. "You two are bumping uglies when we go. Good thing, I suppose. You look like you need it."

He knew? My face flushed hot. "I look like I need it? What does that mean?"

He glanced at Devin.

"Don't look at me," Devin said with a laugh.

"You look uptight," Frank said apologetically.

I cocked my hip. "Uptight?"

He patted my shoulder with his massive hand. "Just a little."

How did Frank know we planned to "bump uglies"? What about me looked uptight? Did others see me that way? Red-faced, I stared, wondering about the answers. As I stood before them, looking uptight, the two men shared a light laugh at my expense.

A moment later, Frank and Shane bid their farewells, agreeing to return in a few days to start the project. As their truck drove away, I realized what was likely going to happen as soon as the door was closed. In the thirty minutes that we'd wasted, I'd floated back down to earth from the euphoric cloud I'd been perched on. Uncertain of how—or if—to proceed along the same lines as before, I pulled the door closed and checked my nails.

"Grab your purse," Devin said. "Let's go."

My eyes shot from an errant cuticle to him. "Excuse me?"

He gestured to my purse. "Let's go."

"Go? I thought. But. We were," I stammered. "We were going to—"

He shook his head lightly. "Changed my mind."

Sixty seconds earlier, I was undecided. Now I wanted to fuck.

I gave him a condescending look. "Changed your mind?"

He brushed past me. "Yep."

I glared as he sauntered toward the kitchen. When he was out of my eyesight, I rushed after him. I stormed into the doorway and put my hands on my hips.

"What do you mean you changed your mind?" I spat. "What is your deal?"

He opened the refrigerator and removed a bottle of wine. "You brought wine?" I asked.

He dropped it into his weathered leather satchel and turned around. "I did."

It was Friday night. A few glasses of wine and a mile of dick eight inches at a time would be a perfect night.

"What's different between now and thirty minutes ago?" I asked, nearly pleading with him to reconsider.

He stepped to three feet in front of me and gazed into my hopeful eyes. "Look. I came here to do two things. One, I wanted to get a good price on the flooring. Two, I wanted to grudge-fuck you until you couldn't walk out of here. I got the first one—"

"We can do the other," I blurted. "Wait." I gave him a confused look. "Grudge-fuck? Because of what I said in that meeting?"

"More or less."

"Okay, fine. Grudge-fuck me." I wagged my brows. "Sounds fun."

Waiting for me to unblock the doorway, he looked me over. "Too late for that," he said dryly.

"Too late? It's barely past six."

"I was going to grudge-fuck you because you were an irritating bitch," he said flatly. "Now? After being around you for a bit? I've changed my mind."

I wondered what I did to piss him off so much that he wouldn't even grudge-fuck me. I quickly ran through everything that had happened and came up short.

"What did I do?" I asked.

"Nothing," he said. "I just decided I kind of like you."

My face flashed hot. I hoped he couldn't tell, but I was

sure he could. "Oh," I said snidely. "So now you don't want to get your little feelers hurt."

He took the one step that separated us and pressed his massive chest against mine. A faint hint of his cologne mixed with the aroma of his manly musk.

I nearly melted into a puddle at his feet.

He peered into my eyes. "If your pussy's half as good as your tits, your ass, or your pretty little face, fucking it once isn't going to be enough. It's not a risk I'm willing to take." He pushed his way past me and strode toward the door. "Don't forget your purse."

CHAPTER NINE

DEVIN

I'd spent the night wondering if my decision to walk away from Teddi was a good one. I desperately desired her, but I feared the aftermath. If my past "relationships" were any indication, she'd eventually get fed up with my antics and run as fast and as far as she was able.

For some men, aggressive sex followed a night of drinking. For others, it was a means of controlling their sexual partner. Slow, soft, sensual sex had never been an option for me. In fact, I couldn't achieve an erection without having a fistful of a woman's hair in my hand.

Eventually, my sexual requirements grew old with my partners. It wasn't surprising. Deep within my being, I yearned to one day be normal. Sadly, I knew that day would never come.

Unable to sleep, I sat at the kitchen table, sipping my coffee and wondering why I was different from most men.

Herb entered the kitchen, paused, and gave me a confused look. "What in the hell are you doing up at the ass crack of dawn on a Saturday morning?"

"Couldn't sleep."

"Surprising, considering how late you came in last night."

"I went for a ride."

"To where? Miami? Go to see your hooligan friends?"

"Tampa. Rode up there, got some tacos at an all-night stand, and rode back."

"Two hundred miles for a taco?" He shuffled to the coffeepot and poured a cup. "That makes perfect sense."

"Did to me."

"Everything all right?"

"Not especially."

"Want to talk about it?"

"Not especially."

He sat down. "You know, early in our marriage, Midge and I had a parrot. Damned thing could only say one thing. *Hello*. It said it over, and over, and over. After about ten years, it died. It was supposed to live thirty. I told the missus it died from boredom, because all it did was repeat itself. Keep saying 'not especially' for a few more years, and I'll predict an untimely death."

"Go to hell, old man."

He chuckled. "I'm headed that direction. Just give me time."

I laughed. "Sorry if I woke you when I got home."

"I heard you come in, but I fell right back to sleep. You've got distinctive footsteps. As soon as I hear 'em, I relax."

It was four thirty in the morning when I got home. Being up all night wasn't constructive, but I had to do something to keep my mind off Teddi.

"I need to figure out something constructive to do with my day," I said.

"You've already got something to do."

"Do I?"

"Vinnie found out about your coworker gal's ex-boyfriend." He sipped his coffee. "He's in Bonita Springs, five minutes away."

I appreciated the old man's efforts, but I had my doubts that Herb's card-playing buddy found the right person between card games and free cups of coffee at the clubhouse.

I finished my coffee and stood. "I doubt he's got the right guy."

"I don't give a damn if you believe me or not," Herb snarled. "But if Vinnie said it's so, it's so."

I sauntered to the coffeepot. "So Vinnie's a detective now?"

"Better detective than you," he insisted. "That's for damned sure."

I poured a fresh cup and returned to the table. "How does he know it's him?"

"Well, if you'd shut up long enough for me to finish a sentence, I'll show you."

Herb shuffled to the back of the house and returned with his phone. He handed it to me. "Open up the text message thing. There's a picture in there somewhere. I know the son of a bitch is there. I just don't know how to get to it."

I swiped my thumb across the screen, surprised that the old man didn't have a password. I tapped my finger against the text message icon. Two text message threads opened. The first, from Verizon, included offers for a new phone that began two hours prior and dated back years. The other was a message from an out-of-state number that must have been Vinnie's. It had two photos attached to it and an address in Bonita Springs. The photos were of Kate and the same man.

He wasn't what I expected. Not really. A scruffy-looking guy with a deep tan and a sparse, unkempt beard, he looked like he should be living under a bridge.

The photos were taken at two different times in Kate's life, as her hair was colored a little differently in each of the photos.

"How do I know this isn't her brother?" I asked.

"It's on his Facebooks. Vin said there's messages on there about them doing stuff together." He gestured toward the phone. "In that one, they were at the Mercato. Vin said it was some sort of celebration. Grand opening of an Italian joint or something."

"Josh Jackson, huh?"

"That's what he said." He wagged his wrinkled finger at the phone. "It's right there in the message. I saw it late in the evening, yesterday, while you were fucking around in Tampa Bay eating tacos. You can call that phone number, and Vinnie can guide you to that kid's Facebooks."

"Book," I said. "Book. It's not plural. Face*book*. Not books."

"Well la-tee-dah. Fine. Facebook. I don't give a shit what it's called. Scribble down that phone number and call Vinnie. Or send him one of those messages." He scowled. "He's all up-to-date on that shit."

I pulled my phone from my pocket and logged into Facebook. A quick search for "Josh Jackson in Bonita Beach, Florida" produced the guy's profile. After a few minutes of scrolling through pictures of him with other women, I reached the point in his timeline where he and Kate were obviously together.

He wasn't her brother, that much I was sure of.

The photos—at least some of them—were seven months old, which coincided with Kate's comment of the relationship ending six months prior.

Seeking revenge on the man who hit Kate would be a perfect way for me to rid myself of my frustrations. I turned off my phone and peered across the table. "Looks like Vinnie's right."

"Well, hell." He chuckled a dry laugh. "That didn't take long. You a computer hacker in a former life?"

"All I needed was a name."

"You can just go to someone's Facebook and look at everything? Just like that?"

"More or less."

His wiry brows pinched together. "That's dumber'n fuck."

I laughed. "Why?"

"Be like taking the family photo album to the clubhouse and just leaving it there for everyone to peruse through. That stuff's personal, and it ought to stay that way. Isn't anyone's business what I'm doing or who I'm screwing. Putting everything out there for the world to see doesn't do anything but open a man up to criticism. Keeps denial from being a plausible option, too." He motioned to my phone. "Just like that dumbass. If his pictures weren't all out there for the world to see, he could deny it. Kind of tough now, ain't it?"

"Sure is."

"So, what are we going to do?" he asked.

"*We* aren't going to do anything. I'm going to pay him a visit." I glanced at my watch. It was six a.m. I looked at Herb with apologetic eyes. "I'll probably head that direction right now."

"Bullshit," he snapped back. "Vinnie and I are going too. You go rolling up to his place on that raggedy-assed Harley all covered in tattoos, and the jig'll be up for sure. We all go up there in Vin's Cadillac, and he's gonna wonder what the hell we want. I guarantee you he'll open the door for two old men and an idiot biker."

I hated to admit it, but Herb was right. I was in top physical condition and covered in tattoos. The layman's perception of me would be that I was a thug. If I knocked on his door alone, he wouldn't answer.

"Fine," I said. "Call Vinnie and see if he's up and ready. We should do it soon. Maybe try to get there by six thirty, before he leaves for the day."

"He's up at four thirty, just like me."

"Well, get him over here," I said. "And we'll get this show on the road."

★ ★ ★

After stopping at the Dunkin' Donuts for a cup of coffee and a pastry, we made it to Josh's house just before seven a.m.

I followed Vinnie and Herb to the front door. The home was a modest ranch with a one-car garage in a quiet neighborhood positioned in the center of town. Despite the faded exterior paint and damaged roof tiles, the yard was well-kept and landscaped beautifully. The garage door was closed, and no cars were parked in the drive, leading me to believe there were no Friday night visitors still occupying the home.

Herb was dressed in a pair of khaki-colored old-man pants and a powder-blue, short-sleeved button-down shirt that was tucked tightly into his waistline. He looked like every other eighty-year-old man in Southwest Florida.

Vinnie wasn't quite what I expected. In his mid-sixties, by my guess, he was five-foot-six or so, built like a semi-retired weightlifter, and had a thick New Jersey accent. He wore his salt-and-pepper hair slicked back, and he walked with a noticeable "don't fuck with me" gait.

He was dressed like he was headed to a nightclub. Two gold chains dangled from his thick neck, one of which had a large, diamond-encrusted crucifix. A gold Rolex watch was on his left wrist, and his right was adorned with a gold chain. Several of his fingers, including his right pinkie, were fitted with gaudy gold rings. Wearing a pair of olive-colored slacks, black dress shoes, and an untucked black silk shirt, he looked the part of a stereotypical East Coast mobster.

When we reached the front door, Vinnie nudged his way in front of Herb. He glanced at me. "Pay attention."

"To what?" I asked.

We'd agreed the two old men would lure Josh to answer the door, with me hidden out of view. Once the door was open, I'd take it from there, pushing him back inside the home to take care of business. After I made myself clear, we'd depart with a stern warning of retaliation if he spoke to police regarding the incident or to Kate about anything.

Vinnie slammed the backside of his thick fist against the door like he was a detective serving a warrant.

"What's with the cop knock?" I whispered.

He glanced over his shoulder and shot me a glare.

He knocked again. This time it was much harder than the first.

"Jesus," I said.

The same "go fuck yourself" glare followed.

Herb teetered back and forth on the balls of his feet nervously. I felt like an extra in a scene from a Martin Scorsese mobster movie, with Vinnie playing the lead, Herb along for the ride, and me as a stand-in.

The door opened a few inches. From my position, I couldn't see a thing.

"What, umm," a tired voice stammered. "Is there something—"

Vinnie planted the heel of his shoe against the door with such force that it slammed against the face of whoever was peering through it.

"Fuckin' piece of fuckin' shit," Vinnie seethed, storming through the opening.

I edged my way past Herb and stepped inside the home. Josh's left hand was in front of his face, covering his eye. Wearing sweatpants and a wrinkled T-shirt, it was obvious he'd just crawled out of bed.

He looked at Vinnie through one extremely wide eye. "What the—"

"Fuckin' *stronzo*. I ought to cut yah fuckin' hands off," Vinnie snarled. He kicked the toe of his shoe against Josh's shin, just below the knee.

Josh fell to the floor like someone had pushed him off a cliff. "Goddammit," he whined, looking up with his one good eye. He glanced at me and then Herb. "Who the fuck—"

"Hit a fuckin' woman?" Vinnie asked. "In the face? *Che palle?*"

Josh's eyes shifted from Herb to Vinnie.

The heel of Vinnie's shoe came crashing down against Josh's stomach. Repeatedly, Vinnie stomped until Josh was wadded into a tight ball.

Assuming it was over, I nudged my way to Vinnie's side. He looked at me with anger-filled eyes. Holding my gaze, he stomped his heel against the side of Josh's face.

Blood ran along the side of Josh's face and pooled on the floor. A large gash on his upper cheek would require a dozen or more stitches. The ugly scar would act as a reminder of the mistakes he'd made.

"Katelyn Winslow," Vinnie said. He tapped the toe of his bloody shoe against Josh's temple until Josh looked up. "Ever talk to her again, I'll come back here and cut yah cock off, yah fuckin' *medigan*." Satisfied that he'd done the damage he'd come to administer, Vinnie leaned over Josh and spat onto his bloody face. "*Vaffanculo!*"

He looked at me. "He's all yaws, kid."

It had only taken Vinnie thirty seconds to take care of Josh, but he'd done so quite authoritatively. I really had no idea what I could add to make our visit any more memorable.

"This happened because you punched Katelyn in the face," I said. "Don't ever approach her, message her, talk to her, or attempt to make contact with her in any way, shape, or form. If you do, I'll be back. If you talk to the police, I'll be back. If I ever hear of you touching another woman in a derogatory manner, I'll be back. The next time I come back, I'm not bringing two nice old men with me. I'm bringing a dozen outlaw bikers." I raised my brows. "Are we clear?"

Peering up at me through the one eye that wasn't swollen shut, Josh nodded his bloody head.

I raised my right boot over his crotch. "Are we clear?"

"Yes. Understood," he blurted. "I understand."

I stomped the heel of my boot into his crotch. I couldn't leave without doing *something* in retaliation for what he'd done to Kate. It seemed minuscule in comparison to Vinnie's violent rampage, but it would have to suffice.

"C'mon, fellas." I turned away and stepped through the

door. "I'll buy the coffee."

Herb pushed me out of the way and shuffled to Josh's side. He kicked him in the ribs. "Don't." He kicked him again. "Hit." He kicked him again. "Women."

He spat on the floor beside him and turned toward the door.

I patted Herb on the shoulder. "Good job, old man."

We got inside Vinnie's Cadillac. With me seated in the back seat and Vinnie and Herb in the front, we pulled away from the curb like we were leaving a funeral. Seeming to be completely over his fit of anger, Vinnie crept up the street at a snail's pace.

He adjusted the rearview mirror so he could see my reflection. "Herb tells me youz got an Italian home on the beach for sale."

"We do. It'll be finished next week. It's more of a mansion than a home, though."

"When can we see it?" he asked.

Vinnie lived in Herb's neighborhood, Pelican Bay. It was a gated community that butted against a private beach. A mixture of condos, single-family homes, and duplexes intended for the elderly, it was an expensive place to live by anyone's standards. It wasn't, however, sixty million dollars' worth of expensive.

"Did he tell you what we were asking for it?"

"Sixty?"

"Million," I said.

"Yah don't fuckin' say," he said in a snide tone. "I thought youz were gonna take sixty bucks for the bastahd."

I shrugged. "Just thought I'd make it clear."

He glanced into the mirror. "Yah think I'm a fuckin' *gidrul*?"

I didn't know what it meant, but I was sure it wasn't good. I shook my head. "No."

"I know people who know people who might have a little fuckin' money they need to spend," he said. "Set up a time for me to see the fuckin' place, would ya?"

I laughed at the thought of Teddi meeting Vinnie. "Sure thing, Vinnie," I said with a laugh. "I'll set it up."

CHAPTER TEN

TEDDI

Monday mornings were bad by design. Monday mornings filled with thoughts of rejection were much worse.

I'd spent the entire weekend sobbing. Although Devin inspired my emotional meltdown, it certainly wasn't his fault. His decision to deny me sex was merely the straw that broke the camel's back.

A lifetime of trusting the wrong men, being used, and putting faith where it didn't belong came to an ugly head. To cope—or to keep from coping—I guzzled wine and binge-watched rom-coms on Netflix for the entire weekend.

Convinced my relationship woes were by my own making, I stumbled into the office hungover and tired. Wearing sunglasses to hide my puffy eyes, I strolled toward Devin's workstation, convinced I could walk past without so much as looking at him.

Just through the door, I looked up. Devin was standing at his desk, stretching his arms. A few days' growth of beard covered his angular jaw. His pressed shirt clung tightly to his wide chest. The outline of his muscular biceps was draped by his shirt's sleeves, but little was left to the imagination.

I admired him as I strolled toward his desk, wondering if his weekend was as gut-wrenching as mine.

"Good morning," he said as I approached. "How was your weekend?"

My lips parted slightly. I wanted to speak. To tell him how much it hurt to be rejected. Explain what it was like to feel there was something wrong with me. To know deep within my heart of hearts that when I decided to give myself to a man, it would only be a matter of days, weeks, or months before I was reminded that relationships, for whatever reason, simply didn't work out for me.

Brimming with emotion, I strolled past him without so much as acknowledging his presence. After making a cup of coffee, I sat in my office and stared at the door. Knowing he was fifty feet from where I was sitting—but that I couldn't even bring myself to talk to him—ground against my every nerve.

I picked up my phone's receiver and dialed Kate's extension.

"Good morning," she said upon answering.

"Get in here."

"Be right there."

The receiver no more than fell into the cradle, and Kate ducked through the door. "Spent the weekend not answering calls and texts. I'm guessing it was a good one?"

"Shut the door."

She shut the door and took a seat on the other side of my desk. "Sunglasses are a nice touch. Were you up all night with you know who?"

I removed them and tossed them into my purse.

"Oh, no," she said. "What happened?"

I pressed my fingertips against the skin beneath my eyes. "Is it that bad?"

She leaned against the edge of my desk and looked me

over. "You look like you spent the entire weekend crying."

"That's because I spent the entire weekend crying."

She relaxed in her chair. "Start at the beginning."

"The beginning?"

"Uh-huh."

"I think it must have started when my parents were killed. Not having them around to give reassurances left me hoping to find it from men. I've been so eager to get someone to pat me on the back that I've made some ridiculously bad decisions."

"Not that beginning," she said. "On Friday. What happened?"

"Oh, God." I rolled my eyes. "It was awful."

"Details, dear. Details."

"We went to the house, and he was showing me the floor. When he stood up, he pinned me to the wall and said, 'I want you to decide if you want me to fuck you or not. I can't decide for you.' It was right at the same time the men showed up to look the place over. They rang the doorbell—"

"Wait. He pinned you to the wall? Like, explain that, would you?"

"Pinned me to the wall, Kate. He pressed his chest against mine, forcing me against the wall. Our lips were basically touching. Basically."

"Did he kiss you?"

"No. He just said the you-have-to-decide thing."

"Okay." She wagged her brows. "Continue."

"They came and looked the place over, and he was eyeing me the entire time. Saying little things, and—"

"What kind of little things?"

"Jeez, Kate, I don't know. *Things.* Little sexual things. And he was looking at me with those eyes. His eyes." I leaned forward. "Have you spent any time looking at his eyes?"

She nodded in agreement. "He's got good eyes, that's for sure."

"Well, he kept looking at me. Saying things. I'm waiting for his two friends to leave, knowing when they do that he's going to bend me over that island in the kitchen and have his way with me. He brought wine, Kate. He put a bottle of wine in that worn-out little leather messenger bag he carries."

"At what point did it go to hell?" she asked. "Was the sex bad?"

"There was no sex."

"What?" she screeched. "How in the world?"

"When they left, he went into the kitchen, grabbed the wine, and pinned me to the wall again. He told me I had a nice ass, nice tits, and a pretty face, but that my pussy might be too pretty to fuck."

Her eyes thinned to slits. "What. Does. That. Even. Mean?"

"I know, right? I have no idea."

"He said you've got a cooch too cute to copulate." She laughed. "Then what did he do?"

"Basically, he shoved me out of his way and stomped out to the car."

"That's it?" she snapped back. "No nothing?"

"Nope."

"What about Saturday?"

"I spent the weekend watching rom-coms on Netflix and crying. He took his shirt off, by the way. That was interesting."

"Wait. What? Took his shirt off? When?"

"Before he pinned me to the wall."

"Just ripped off his shirt and smashed you to the wall?"

"Basically, yeah."

"Holy crap," she gasped. "Then, nothing?"

"He's so sexy it makes me sick," I said. "I can't do this."

"Do what?"

"Spend every waking hour wanting him. I don't know what it is about him, but I want him so bad it hurts."

She waved her hand in the direction of his desk. "Go tell him you've got an ugly twat. Maybe he'll reconsider."

"That's not funny."

"It was kind of funny." She brushed the wrinkles from her dress. "What did he look like without his shirt on?"

"What do you think?" I asked. "He looked like someone ought to be chiseling a statue of his likeness and placing it in Naples Park."

"I want this to work," she said.

"You want what to work?"

"This. You. Him. This."

I glared. "You little turd. This is your fault. You basically set me up."

She cowered in her seat, but it was only an act. "I may have planted a seed or two," she admitted. "A few in his head, a few in yours."

I shook my head in disgust. "Well, your little plan didn't work."

"He's perfect for you," she said. "He's a sexual deviant, and so are you. He's loyal, and so are you. He's alpha, and you're subservient."

"I'm *not* subservient," I snapped. "I can't believe you said that."

She stood, walked around the corner of my desk, and got on my computer. After a few seconds of typing, she gestured to the screen. "Read it."

sub·ser·vi·ent / sәb 'sәrvēәnt - *adjective* - *willing and eager to obey another unquestioningly – "She was subservient to her partner."*

"Maybe a little bit," I said. "But it doesn't matter. It's never going to work."

"A little bit." She laughed. "You define the term."

"I do not."

"If he walked in here right now and said, 'Bend over that desk. I want to fuck you from behind,' or whatever, you'd do it."

"I would not," I said adamantly. "One, I wouldn't have sex in my office. Two, he couldn't just order me around like that."

"Yes, he could."

"Maybe a little, but not in here. My office is my sanctuary. This place is off-limits."

"Well, my point was that you two are perfect for each other. I hate to admit it, but that's the reason I hired him. Not the entire reason, but it was a big part of it."

I was flattered and pissed off all at the same time. "Are you kidding me?" I asked, my tone laced with aggravation. "You hired him because you thought—"

"I hired him because I'm tired of seeing you in pain. You deserve so much better than you've received. I hired him because he was willing, qualified, and because he said he'd stay long-term. My hope was that you two would hit it off. After I figured out who he was and what he stood for, I decided I had to put you two together."

"What does he stand for?" I asked.

"He's a good man, and he stands up for women at any and all costs."

"I wish he wanted me as much as I want him."

"Let me see if I can fix this," she said.

"Leave it alone," I insisted. "I only want him if he wants me. If he's doing you a favor, it's just not the same."

She stood and gestured toward my purse. "Put your sunglasses on, dear. You look like hell."

My eyes were swollen, my heart hurt, and the only man who came within inches of wanting me in the past year was a disastrous setup from a friend and coworker who felt sorry for me.

I not only looked like hell, I felt like it, too.

"I'll leave them off," I said. "I deserve this."

"You do not," she insisted. "You deserve the best."

I might have deserved it, but I had my doubts I'd ever receive it.

CHAPTER ELEVEN

DEVIN

Kate and I were seated at a coffee shop having a caffeinated beverage and a light dinner to celebrate my two-week anniversary with the company.

"I like this place a latte," she said.

I couldn't help but laugh. "Me too."

Kate was exactly what I needed in a friend. She kept conversations interesting, didn't muddy up our friendship waters with drama, and always wore a smile. In the past, my friends had been limited to men who were constantly in a state of competition with one another. Trying to go faster, outdrink, or earn more money than the man next to them. It was a breath of fresh air to have someone who wanted nothing more than to enjoy my company.

"So, do you have any idea what's wrong with Teddi lately?" She sipped her latte. "Every time I've seen her this week, she's been really short with me."

Since I denied her sexual requests, Teddi hadn't spoken more than two words to me. I didn't know her well enough to decide if her patterns of coming and going were normal, but short of a few silent trips past me to get something from her desk, she'd avoided me like the plague.

I hated that things had changed between us. Teddi didn't

know it, but I was saving her from a mountain of grief. She could be pissed off all she wanted, but I wasn't going to be a selfish prick and ruin her image of me all for a few nights of sex.

"Probably stressed out about the house," I replied.

"I suppose that could be it," she said, seeming far from convinced.

I decided to change the subject. "The house should be done by the end of next week, by the way."

"Oh, wow. Those guys work fast."

"They'd be a lot faster if I didn't have them do a little extra work."

She lowered her cup to the table and picked up her biscotti. She looked it over as if trying to decide where to sink her teeth. "You don't think Teddi's attitude could have something to do with the fact that you wouldn't have sex with her, do you?"

I choked on my espresso. A teary-eyed coughing fit followed. When I caught my breath, I looked at her with eyes of disbelief. "She told you?"

She dunked her biscotti in her coffee and nodded eagerly. "She's devastated."

"Devastated?"

"Absolutely crushed," she said over a mouthful of biscotti. "Things like that have a profound effect on women."

"Believe me, I had no intention of causing her that kind of grief. My experience in dealing with women's emotions is nil. I had no idea—"

"This is why we're friends." She pointed the uneven tip of her biscotti at me. "I can teach you such things."

"Why would not having sex be so devastating?" I asked. "It doesn't make sense that she's pissed about something so stupid."

"I doubt she saw it as stupid."

"We were going to fuck," I said dismissively. "We didn't. It wasn't a big deal."

"The last guy..." She paused and looked me over. "Can I tell you about the last guy she saw without you telling her I told you?"

"Sure."

"The last guy she saw was over a year ago. They were serious. Living together and everything. She heard he was having sex with another woman. She asked him. He denied it. Then, someone hinted that there was another. She asked him again, and he denied it. It went on for a long time. The accusations and the denials. Then, one day, she caught him."

"How?"

"He worked for us." A look of disgust washed over her. She shook her head. "This is awful. She met a woman at one of his listings because he was in Orlando at some meeting, or training, or whatever. Anyway, this client started telling Teddi how she was seeing this guy. She was buying this house, and he was going to move in with her. It ended up the guy this client was seeing was the same guy Teddi was living with. It messed her up pretty bad."

"Guy sounds like a real shithead," I said.

"There's a lot more to it than that."

"More than him being a shithead?"

"No," she said. "More to the story."

"Are you going to tell it?"

She seemed reluctant but continued nonetheless. "She'd given him almost every penny she saved to help finance some real estate thing. It was a lot of money. The investment scheme was basically a scam. It ended up that was really the only reason he was with her. For her money. She lost it all. Every cent. After that, she swore off guys, basically."

"Holy shit. Where's this guy now? In prison?"

"No. She didn't prosecute him. She was too embarrassed. He's working for another real estate agency here in town."

"You're kidding?"

"I wish I was."

"That's awful." I exhaled a long breath. "Both parts to the story."

"Now you know why it was a big deal to her. If she made up her mind to have sex with you, she reached a point she'd overcome everything with the guy who screwed her over. It was probably a big letdown. Then she was left wondering if she made the right decision or if all guys are turds."

"I'm not a turd."

"I'm not saying you are. I'm just kind of thinking out loud. Trying to decide what she's thinking."

"The asshole who took her money. He's here? In Naples?"

"He is."

"What's his name?"

She shook her head. "Sorry. I'm not telling you that."

"Why not?"

"Because. I don't want you to go back to prison any more than you want to be there."

I wasn't going to risk going to prison over it. I just wanted to know. I waved it off. "I'm just curious. No big deal."

She gnawed on her biscotti like a starving hamster. Halfway through it, she appeared to have a revelation. "Oh crap. I just remembered something."

I glanced at my watch. "Do you have to go?"

"No. It was about that other thing we talked about."

"What other thing?"

"About you being a sexual misfit. Remember, I told you I was going to find someone who qualified? Someone who would match your sexual personality?"

"Oh. Yeah." I finished my espresso in one gulp. "No such luck, huh?"

"Not really," she said. "Just one person. I doubt you'll be interested."

"Is she like me?"

"Probably more of a misfit, really."

It sounded like a match made in heaven. My eyes widened with wonder. "Oh, really?"

"Yeah," she said with a laugh. "I'm sure she'd teach you a thing or two."

"I doubt it."

"I don't," she said matter-of-factly.

I wished things with Teddi were different. I couldn't stop thinking about her. Finding the right person would be both rewarding and painful. Being in a relationship while working with Teddi would do nothing but cause her pain, and that wasn't something I wanted to do.

"Who is it?" I asked out of sheer curiosity.

She smiled. "Teddi."

CHAPTER TWELVE

TEDDI

I rummaged through the documents scattered across my desk. Immersed in my efforts to find a contract, I'd become immune to my surroundings. The sound of someone clearing their throat snatched me from my focused state.

Cringing, I looked up.

A few feet from my desk, Devin stood with his hands in his pockets. "Got a minute?"

I'd stopped in just for a moment, hoping I could retrieve the documents without being cornered. I couldn't have been so lucky. Especially when it came to encountering Devin. I'd managed to avoid him for nearly a week. Merely seeing him brought me grief.

"I need to run," I replied, trying to sound like I was in a hurry. "Can you get with Kate on whatever it is you need?"

"I can't."

I grabbed my purse. "I'm sorry. I've got—"

He gave me a soft look. "I'm sorry."

I paused. "About what?"

"The other night."

What happened between the two of us was simple. I was attracted to him. I opened up, sexually. I offered myself to him. He rejected me. That should have been the end of it. Oddly, it seemed to be only the beginning.

My desire to be with him had increased exponentially since the rejection. I'd never been so attracted to anyone in my life. To have him reject me was crushing. An apology did nothing to change how I felt. I wanted him to want me as much as I wanted him.

I adjusted my shoulder strap. "Okay."

"Is there a way we can start over?"

Devin had no desire to be with me, even if only for a one-time sexual encounter. Whenever I saw him, heard his voice, or Kate mentioned him, it was a reminder of that. "Starting over" meant that he wanted to patch things up between us. He'd expect me to stop by his workstation and chat. Have lunch with him and Kate. An after-work drink. Emotionally, I wasn't ready. Maybe I would be one day, but I wasn't there yet.

"I don't think we need to start over," I said, trying to walk past him. "I'm sorry. I really need to get—"

"Stop." He reached for my waist. "Please."

I wanted to scream. To tell him to get his hands off me. Instead, I stood statue-still and said nothing. As I savored the feeling of having him touch me, I closed my eyes.

"I wish I could rewind the clock and do things differently," he said. "But I can't."

He was pouring salt on my wounds. To hear that everything was a mistake would only make matters worse. I needed to stop him from continuing. I opened my eyes. Before I spoke, he continued.

"I want to do this," he said.

My mind swam in a sea of confusion. I blinked a few times and shook my head, hoping to clear it of the fog.

"Do what?" I asked.

"You and me," he replied. "Not one time. Not just sex." He lifted my chin with his finger until our eyes met. "I want to do this."

He kissed me.

It wasn't an indecisive peck on the lips. Nor was it an "I don't know what I want" kiss. It wasn't a "hey, I'm sorry for what I've done, please forgive me" kiss, either.

It was an "I want to make sure you know who's in charge" kiss.

He slid his hands down the small of my back and brought them to rest on my ass. He squeezed it like he owned it. I fumbled for a place to put my hands, eventually sinking my fingers into the backs of his firm triceps.

Our tongues intertwined. Our bodies melded together. Kissing him in return as aggressively as he kissed me, I stumbled to maintain my footing. We collided with the desk. Our lips parted. I looked at him, and he at me.

Desire radiated from his eyes.

He swept my desk clean with one brisk wave of his arm. Contracts, books, papers, office supplies—everything—clattered across the hardwood floor.

He turned me around and pushed me facedown onto the desk. "Tell me you want this," he said, pressing his hand between my shoulder blades. "Say it, you sexy little bitch."

The side of my face was flat on my desk. My legs were tensed with anticipation. "I want it," I said in a shaking voice. "Please. Give it to me."

He flipped my dress over my waist. Then, he did just as I'd daydreamed. He kicked the toe of his boot against the inside edges of my shoes, forcing me to widen my stance.

"Spread 'em wide," he growled.

I did as he asked.

He leaned over, pressing his chest tight against my back. He positioned his mouth beside my ear.

"Don't move," he breathed.

I stood, motionless. A pronounced metallic *click* caused me to tense.

While he continued to breathe into my ear, he cut each side of my panties in two at my hips. They fluttered to the floor. The air escaped my lungs in an uneven breath.

I heard him fumble with his belt buckle. The sound of him tearing a condom from the package followed. I ached with anticipation. He pressed his hand against the back of my head, forcing my cheek firmly onto the cold surface of the desk.

"Tell me to fuck you," he demanded. "Say it."

"Oh my God." I gasped. "Fuck me. Fuck me. Jesus. Fuck me."

I wanted to see his cock. His face. His body. But I didn't dare attempt to raise my head. I focused my eyes on the far wall, thankful that my door was closed. I felt pressure against my wet folds. Then he began to penetrate me, slowly.

As his massive length entered me, I inhaled a choppy breath. His cock seemed to be endless, touching places inside me I never knew existed.

The tip bumped my cervix.

"Holy shit," I said on the heels of an exhaled breath. "That feels so good."

I was no newcomer to sex, but this was different. His length, girth, and his processes were far beyond what I was accustomed to.

Holding himself inside me, he leaned forward until his body covered mine completely. I felt his warm breath against my ear.

"I'm going to make you come," he said in a low growl. "When you do, you're going to scream."

If I screamed, the entire office would know what was going on—if they didn't already.

"If I scream—"

"When you do, you're going to scream," he insisted, whispering through clenched teeth. He glanced at his watch. "You've got three minutes to accomplish it. Are you ready?"

Three minutes?

What the fuck?

I knew better than to argue with either point.

"Okay," I said.

One hand pressed against my back. The other held a fistful of my hair as it forced my face firmly onto the desk.

His hips slapped against my ass, sending an unmistakable clapping sound echoing throughout my office with each savage stroke. One immediately after the other, they came, *bam! bam! bam!* Each one forcing my thighs against the edge of the desk.

"You. Sexy. Little. Bitch. I. Love. Your. Tight. Little. Pussy," he said, saying one word with each instroke.

I had no idea what his cock looked like, but if it were any bigger, I couldn't have accepted it. If it were any smaller, there would have been no chance of me reaching climax in the three-minute window of opportunity he'd given me.

He released the pressure from my head and pulled me upright by my shoulders. With my back arched and his entire length still buried deep in my wetness, he yanked my shirt open, sending buttons flying across the floor.

"I want to squeeze these big fucking titties," he said under his breath.

He pulled my bra down. My breasts lurched out, falling into his waiting hands. He gripped them firmly, squeezing them with his massive palms while tweaking my nipples between his thumbs and forefingers.

I had no idea where we were in respect to time, but I was on the cusp of climax.

Holding me in place by my boobs, he pressed his chest against my back and continued his sexual advances, pounding himself into my memory bank one ferocious stroke at a time. Lost in the rhythmic sensation of his scrotum smacking against my clit, I closed my eyes and clenched my teeth.

My body tensed.

"I'm going to come," I announced.

He continued the same predictable pace, not breaking his rhythm. I arched my back and opened my eyes wide.

He sank his teeth into the base of my neck. "Come, you sexy little bitch," he muttered against my flesh. "Come."

I was already on the brink. As with everything else he'd asked of me, I complied. I relaxed and closed my eyes. My everything began to tingle.

My pussy clenched his swollen shaft.

"Oh my God," I wailed. "Keep going. Keep going. Yes. Yes. Yes."

My entire body shuddered from the shock of his continued thrusts. Each one sent another surge of electricity from my scalp to my toes.

His cock swelled, bringing me to yet another orgasm. This one was much deeper and stronger, taking every bit of energy from me as it filled me with euphoric bliss.

"Holy fuuuuuck!" I bellowed.

When the orgasm subsided, I collapsed against the desk. I spent several moments collecting my thoughts. I aimlessly looked around the office. On the floor beside me, my panties were ruined. Beyond them, buttons were scattered about. Like seashells along the sandy beach, they peppered the floor of my office.

Resting his weight against my back was none other than Devin "Bone" Wallace, a man I deeply desired and, for some reason, yearned to satisfy.

"How'd I do?" I asked.

He slid his hand beneath my head and lifted it from the desk. He looked me in the eyes and smiled. "You did great," he said. "I'm proud of you."

He kissed me.

A warm feeling of accomplishment filled me. When our lips parted, I studied his face. I knew very little about him, but I knew one thing, and I knew it for sure.

Quitting him wasn't going to come easily.

CHAPTER THIRTEEN

DEVIN

We sat across from one another at a restaurant's outdoor seating area, half a block off the Tamiami Trail. With covered outdoor seating as the only option, I was reluctant to agree to the order-at-the-window diner. Much to my surprise, the food at the Lake Park Diner was remarkable.

Teddi hadn't changed, but my perception of her did. Following sex with most women, I wanted to disappear. With Teddi, it was the opposite. I couldn't get enough of her. "I like your hair up. It looks nice."

"Thank you. I'll wear it up more often."

"Keep doing what you're doing," I said. "I like how you change it up. It always looks nice. Up, down, that thing you do when the sides are pulled up and the rest is down. I like 'em all."

She touched her bun with her flattened hand. "Thank you."

She studied her sandwich, trying to figure out which end she was going to attack it from. I found it interesting that I perceived her differently now that we were officially "dating." When we first met, I saw her as an attractive woman who had an abrasive—and often rude—personality. Now, I saw her as an attractive woman who was merely trying to protect herself from being harmed emotionally.

The two were worlds apart.

She bit the corner of her sandwich and then took another immediate bite. She looked like an alligator devouring a duck. "This is so freaking good."

A piece of fried chicken protruded from between the slices of toasted bread. I nodded toward it.

"What is it?" I asked.

"Pimento chicken sandwich," she said over a mouthful of food. "Pimento cheese, bacon jam, arugula, and buttermilk fried chicken. It's to die for."

"A fried chicken sandwich?" I narrowed my gaze in disbelief. "Do you always eat like this?"

Midway through another monstrous bite, she paused. She nodded eagerly. "I've got the metabolism of a cheetah."

She didn't have an ounce of fat on her.

"You must," I said with a laugh. "You can't weigh ninety-eight pounds."

"A hundred eighteen, this morning," she said, as if it were a bad thing. "It fluctuates based on my eating habits. I'll go a while eating like this and then feel guilty and stop. Generally, I can get by on wine, coffee, and compliments."

"Compliments? You can't sustain life with compliments."

"I can come close. They go a long way with me. I'm one of those women who constantly needs reassurance that she's doing a good job."

"Have you tried Downtown Coffee and Wine in Bonita?" I asked. "They make a killer espresso. You could get two out of three of your necessities right there."

She swallowed her food and grinned. "I haven't. But wine and coffee in one place? That's genius."

"It's fantastic," I said. "The beverages and the food. Kate introduced me to it."

"If you went with me, I could get coffee, wine, and compliments all in one place. I like how you compliment me, by the way. It's nice."

It was difficult not to compliment her. In my eyes, she defined perfection. I offered her a look of reassurance. "Keep being you, and I'll keep the compliments coming."

"I can't be anyone else." She nibbled her sandwich. "The house will be done tomorrow?"

"It will. I've got quite a surprise for you, too."

Her eyes shot wide. "Now?"

"Not now. Tomorrow, when we see it."

"I can't wait." With her mouth curled into a slight smile, she gazed blankly at me for a moment. "How can you be single?" she asked, going back to inspecting her sandwich. "Or, how could you be single? You're too good a catch to be available."

"I've never been in a serious relationship," I admitted. "Mister perpetually single."

She gave me a funny look. "I don't see you as a player."

I finished my Korean beef taco and wiped my hands clean. "I'm not. When I was young, I figured out that sex didn't really work for me, so I never really had a relationship until I was older. My relationships weren't really relationships, just me seeing someone for a couple of weeks. As soon as they figured out things were the way they were, they'd leave me."

"What do you mean sex didn't work for you?"

"I realized I couldn't get it up if I didn't have a handful of hair or was talking filthy. Not everyone wants to participate in such filth."

"Oh." She wrinkled her nose. "You couldn't achieve erection without it?"

"Nope."

"I'll be darned." She picked up the other half of her sandwich. "It's not filth, by the way. Just because it's different from the norm doesn't mean it's bad. With regular sex or whatever it's called, I never could have done that three-minute thing I did. No way. It would take me an hour to reach climax, if it ever happened."

It was reassuring to think that there was someone else who possessed the same sexual characteristics and desires I did. Whether our relationship lasted three weeks or three months, having a compatible partner was a huge plus.

"So, what about you and relationships?" I asked. "Why are you single?"

She put her sandwich down and sipped her vodka spritzer through the straw. "I've been in a few relationships. The last one was a disaster. I haven't been in one for a year. Gun-shy or whatever after that one, I guess."

"What was disastrous about it?"

"He was a liar," she replied. "And a cheater. And an all-around dick."

"That sucks. Was that the disastrous part? His cheating?"

She picked up her sandwich and then put it down. "It was part of it, yeah."

I hated to press the issue, but I'd promised Kate I wouldn't mention what she'd shared with me. Without Teddi telling me the details, I couldn't discuss it with her.

I picked up another taco and took a small bite. "An all-around dick, huh?" I asked, trying not to act too interested. "Tell me what a guy does to get that label. I'll be sure that I don't make the same mistakes."

"Don't worry, you won't."

"Let's hope not."

She ate half of what remained of her sandwich and pushed the plate aside. After finishing her vodka drink, she raised the empty glass. "These things are so good. If I have another, will you drive?"

"Sure."

She got another drink. While we talked about our favorite local places to eat, she finished it and then got another. Hopeful that all hundred and eighteen pounds of her would be drunk and willing to talk by the time she finished drink number three, I recommended Brooks Burgers as my favorite burger joint.

"It was ranked number two or three in the nation for burgers," I said. "That's quite an accomplishment if you ask me."

"It's a hamburger," she argued. "Hamburgers are boring."

"Most people would think that sparkling water with a shot of vodka and the essence of kiwi fruit dribbled into it is boring. To each their own."

"I like it that we like different things," she said. "I look forward to broadening my eating horizons. Opening up to new things."

"One of these days you're going to have to open up to riding on the back of my motorcycle."

"I don't know about that. Maybe."

The motorcycle wasn't simply a mode of transportation for me. It was part of my being. Without it, I doubted I'd be able to maintain my sanity. "I think you'll like it. I hope you do, anyway. It's a big part of who I am."

She sipped her drink. "What do you mean?"

"It's an escape. A very necessary one. It's like a wonder drug on wheels. Whatever's broken, a ride will fix it."

"I doubt that."

"Don't doubt it until you've at least tried it."

"We'll see," she said.

We'll see was a soft no. "When you're ready, I'll give you a ride. Not until."

"If it'll fix whatever's broken, it sounds like a good idea. If this house sells before the deadline, I'll swallow my reservations and climb on. How's that?"

"I'll hold you to it," I said.

"I'm sure you will." She finished the drink and looked at the empty glass. "I think I'm drunk."

"Do you do this often?" I asked.

"What?"

"Get drunk at lunch?"

"Not really."

"How frequently is *not really*?"

"It's just. When I talk about that last guy I dated, it upsets me. I do this when I get upset. I run from my emotions. I ran the other day when Margaret said she was going to pull the listing, and I'm running now."

"Why don't you try to talk about them? Your emotions... What bothers you?"

"I don't want to be criticized," she said. "I hate rejection. I'd rather keep it all bottled up inside until it eventually goes away."

"What about him upsets you that much?"

"He was screwing half the town." She waved the back of her hand toward the parking lot in the distance. "Maybe more."

"Beating yourself up about it only lets him continue to have control over you. You ended the relationship and walked away. Leave him and everything about him in the past, where it belongs."

"Easy to say, hard to do."

"Why?"

She let out a sigh. "It just is."

"There's a lot about my past that I don't like," I admitted. "I choose not to think about it. It doesn't mean it didn't happen, but it does prevent me from punishing myself repeatedly for it."

"Everyone kept telling me he was screwing around," she said in a barely audible tone. "Every time I asked him, he denied it. Then I met a client at a home he was selling because he was out of town. She started telling me about this guy she was dating. How nice he was. How attractive he was. How perfect he was. In fact, they were moving in together. Into the home she was buying. Guess who her boyfriend was?"

"Your guy?"

"Yeah. I was crushed."

"I'm sure you were," I said. "But he's gone now, and you're undoubtedly better off without him. Let him go. Again, to hold on to the grief is to let him continue to control you. If you're truly disgusted by him, releasing him—and his memories—is the best revenge."

"He took almost...basically, he took...he took everything. He screwed me out of over seven hundred thousand dollars," she said, nearly choking on the words. "It was supposed to be a real estate investment. Some land ownership thing that they were going to build condos on in Marco Island. It never panned out. I'm out the money. My bank account is a constant reminder of him. Letting go isn't that easy."

In my wildest dreams, I wouldn't have imagined it was as bad as it was. The money had to be somewhere. Either he had it, or he had whatever he'd purchased with it. I'd take that up with him when I found him.

"Where's the money?" I asked. "He had to do something with it."

"He was conned out of it." It seemed talking of it was draining the energy from her entirely. Looking defeated, she continued. "We were supposed to be buying into a land deal on Marco, but it fell through. He trusted the wrong people."

There was no doubt someone trusted the wrong person, but I doubted it was him. My guess was that he never invested a dime and used someone else as the scapegoat.

"I'm sorry that happened," I said. "Out of curiosity, where is he now?"

I hated to ask but felt I must. If I hadn't heard the story already through Kate, I would have asked without a second thought.

"He's still selling real estate in town." She met my gaze with glassy eyes. She was on the verge of crying. "He's been in a few times."

"Been in?" I asked. "Where?"

"The office."

My eyes went wide. "Excuse me?"

She dabbed her eyes with her index finger. "He's been in on a few co-listings and when he's sold property I've listed. It sucks, but it's part of it, I guess. He sold one of my listings the other day. He'll be in again soon."

He might have used real estate as an excuse to come into the office in the past, but he wasn't going to do it in the future. Finding him and resolving matters was going to have to happen sooner than I expected.

Seeing her go through such grief was difficult. Knowing she'd have to do it anytime he came into the office made matters much worse.

I reached for her hand. "I need to ask you to trust me, okay?"

She squeezed my hand lightly. "Okay."

"I'm going to take care of this," I assured her. "Believe me. I will. But you're going to have to tell me his name."

"I don't want you to—"

"Listen, Teddi. I like you. A lot. I want to fix this. Trust me when I tell you I can. But you're going to have to tell me his name."

"How are you going to fix it?"

"I'm resourceful."

"Your biker friends?" she asked. "You're going to have them beat him up?"

"No."

"What, then?"

"I look at things this way. You're my responsibility now. To take care of you, I have to take care of this."

"I like being your responsibility." She managed a soft smile. "His name is Britt Wescoff. He's easy to find."

"Thank you." I leaned over the table and gave her a kiss. "You won't regret this."

I hoped like hell I was right.

CHAPTER FOURTEEN

TEDDI

Being blindfolded by a man had been on my wish list for a long time. Being blindfolded and led into one of my listings didn't quite qualify. Holding Devin's hand in mine, I stumbled along the brick drive.

Upon stepping inside, I was met by a faint odor of fresh paint. "It smells like paint."

"I took the liberties to have them do a little painting when they were in here," Devin said. "I hope you like it."

"I hope I do, too," I said, surprised he'd take the initiative to paint without consulting me. After a few more steps, I paused. "Can you take this thing off yet?"

"We're almost there," he said. "I want you to look at it from the kitchen."

Having promised not to visit the home until it was finished, this was the first time I'd seen the interior since the work began almost two weeks earlier. I hoped like hell the changes would allow me to market it to a wide range of clients. I had less than forty days to sell the home and save my career.

I tugged against his hand. "Are we there yet?"

He released me. I felt him fidget with my scarf. Then he pulled it free. When my eyes adjusted to the light, my mouth flopped open. "Oh. My. God."

The hideously dark ornate trim—eight-inch crown and base moldings—had been either replaced or painted. The new color, a beige so light it was almost cream, was a perfect choice for blending with the cabinets and dark marble countertops.

"Good *Oh My God*, or bad *Oh My God*?" he asked.

"Good. Better than good." I alternated glances between him and the newly painted trim. "You had them paint the kitchen? Can they come back and do the rest?"

"The entire house is done. Upstairs. Downstairs. Bedrooms. Bathrooms. It's all done." He gestured to the floor. "Look at the flooring."

The new tile floor was gorgeous. Standing on it and looking down at the product, I would have never guessed it was made of vinyl. My expectations had been exceeded tenfold.

"I want to cry," I said, walking the length of the kitchen. "This is remarkable."

"Before you ask... The paint has to be paid for if the home sells for within ninety-five percent of ask. If it does, it's twelve thousand five hundred. If not, it's free."

"Twelve grand for paint? That's nothing."

"This place will sell now." He looked at me in wonder. "Don't you think?"

"If it doesn't, I'll be shocked," I admitted. "Doing it in less than forty days might be tough."

"Get new pictures taken and do an email blast," he said. "That ought to help."

I laughed. "What do you know about email blasts?"

"More than I should. I've been doing some reading." He put his hands on his hips and admired the work. "I like it."

I didn't like it. I loved it. I looked at him and smiled. "You've got good taste."

He smirked. "Conceited much?"

"I meant the house."

"Oh. Thank you." His gaze floated around the room. "My father used to build homes just like this. Some were thirty-thousand square feet. He didn't actually build them, I guess. He had them built."

I knew his father had passed away, but I didn't know what happened to the company. "Is his company still around?"

"No. It was named Stone-Wall Builders. Cliff Stone and my father, Daniel Wallace. After he died, it became Riverstone or Rambling Stone or something. Cliff retired and sold it a few years ago."

I'd heard of, sold, and admired countless Stone-Wall homes. I couldn't believe it. "Holy shit," I declared. "I bet I've sold more than a dozen of his homes. I had no idea."

His eyes lit up. "Really?"

"Absolutely."

"There's one off Pine Ridge, on that winding street that goes all the way to Lowdermilk Beach..." He rubbed his temples. "I can't think of the name now."

"Crayton?"

"Yeah," he said. "Crayton. I worked on that house when I was in high school, as a carpenter's assistant. It was my first one. I was sixteen."

"Oh, wow. There's some nice homes on Crayton."

"He built several along there. As soon as he got done with one, someone else would want one. They ended up picking up another crew and then another. By the time I was twenty-five, there were three crews going at all times."

"Did you enjoy it?"

"I did."

"Well, there's nothing to say you can't go back sometime."

"For now"—he glanced around the kitchen—"I'll stay right where I am."

I hoped he never left. I realized one day he might, but I didn't want to think about it happening. It seemed like my thoughts of late had been a bunch of ridiculousness, but since our decision to see one another, I'd been happier than I ever remembered being. Admitting it seemed cliché for a woman in a rebound relationship.

"If I've been single for a year, is this a rebound relationship?" I asked.

He shrugged one shoulder. "I don't know what the timeline is for qualifications, but I'd say not."

"Good. I want this relationship to be for all the right reasons."

"I think it is," he said. "We've cleared quite a few hurdles to get here, that's for sure. I was prepared to butt-fuck you just to teach you a lesson after that meeting."

My face flushed. Teaching me a lesson with anal sex as the punishment sounded like a good idea. "Umm. Yeah. You might still need to do that sometime. You'll have to be gentle, though."

He looked me up and down. "Say the word."

"I think I just did."

He glanced around, admiring the work and then met my amorous gaze. "I've got another surprise for you."

I giggled. "You're going to teach me a lesson?"

He laughed. "Not right now, no. I've got a guy who wants to see it."

"See this?" I asked excitedly. "The house?"

"He does. As soon as it's done. I'm not sure of his

qualifications, but he knows what the asking price is, and he wants to see it. I told him we were making updates. He knows today's the day it'll be done."

"Who is he?"

"Vinnie the gangster," he said with a laugh. "He's a Jersey Italian."

"Oh, he'd be perfect," I said. "And you never know with those guys. I had one try to pay me five million for a home in Bonita with a few shoeboxes filled with various denominations of cash."

"Did you do it?" he asked. "Take the cash?"

"Between you and me?" I asked.

"Sure."

"Of course," I replied. "We had to get pretty inventive, but we made it work."

"Just be prepared for a foul-mouthed, over-the-top, in-your-face showing," he said. "This guy's a real piece of work."

"Will you be here?" I asked.

"Actually, I prefer to spearhead the meeting if it's all the same."

It sounded silly to admit, but I was extremely proud of Devin. He'd shown initiative, talent, excellent taste, and considerable knowledge throughout the changes to the listing. I gazed at him admiringly for a moment as he surveyed the home.

"What's the happiest you've ever been?" I asked.

I wanted him to feel the same way I did but felt childish for asking the question. I waited nervously for him to respond.

"Happiest or most satisfied?" he asked, still focused on the home.

"Aren't they the same?"

"I don't think so," he replied, facing me. "Being happy is a joyous state. Being satisfied is more a feeling of contentment. Happy is a stage above satisfied, I guess."

"Okay. Satisfied. When were you the most satisfied?"

His gaze dropped to the floor. After a long period of thought, he lifted his eyes to meet mine. "When I got out of prison."

I wasn't shocked. Not really. I was more surprised that he admitted it to me. "I imagine it was pretty satisfying. It would have to be."

His brow furrowed. "You're not going to ask what I was in for?"

"If you want to tell me, you can."

"I was scared to tell you," he said. "I want this relationship to be transparent, though. I don't want to keep anything from you."

It was a relief to think that someone was going to be honest with me. "Thank you."

He scowled playfully. "I expect the same from you."

"You'll get it."

We toured the home from top to bottom. It looked remarkable from every angle. At the top of the steps, I paused. "Can I have a kiss?"

"Sure." He kissed me twice and then pulled away. "I'm guessing you're happy?"

I laughed to myself. "If you only knew."

He gave me a funny look. "What does that mean?"

"I've never been happier than I am right now," I admitted. "Never."

"In seeing this house?"

"This house is insignificant," I replied. "I'm talking about since you and I started this. You make me happy."

"What about me?"

"It isn't one thing. I like the way you look, the way you act, the way you carry yourself. It's pretty much everything. Yeah. I'll go with that. I like everything about you."

"That's nice to hear," he said, seeming a little embarrassed. "You want to hear something that's going to sound ridiculous?"

"Sure."

"I feel the same way," he said. "About you."

CHAPTER FIFTEEN

DEVIN

Vinnie stepped inside the door. His eyes widened as he took in the grand entrance. He gazed at the twin staircases that flanked the entrance. "*Che figato!*"

"You like it so far?"

His eyes darted from one area to another, taking in everything that was within view. "The *medigan* who had this fuckin' place musta been *nuotare nell'oro.*"

He acted like I spoke his native tongue. I gave him a funny look. "What does that mean?"

"I said the idiot who owned the place musta been swimmin' in fuckin' gold." He waved his hand toward the upstairs handrail as he walked along the hallway. "Look around, would ya? Venetian plastah. Imported mahble. Fuckin' place looks like a million bucks, huh?"

"Sixty," I said with a laugh. "Looks like sixty million bucks."

"I think he likes it," Teddi whispered.

"Whattabout the beach?" he asked, glancing over his shoulder as he walked toward the living room. "Do all these fuhkas along here have beach views?"

"There's a beach view from the entire west side of the house," Teddi said. "Each of the bedrooms and the master bath all have views as well."

He peered through the west-facing sliding glass windows. Beyond the swimming pool, the luscious landscape gave a remote tropical island feel. A few footsteps beyond the yard's final row of palms, the Gulf of Mexico stretched for as far as the eye could see. The deep blue water glistened beneath the afternoon sun.

"That section of beach?" he asked, gesturing to the sand in the distance. "It's the homeownahs?"

"The homeowner?" Teddi asked.

"That's what I said," he said, seeming almost irritated. "The fuckin' homeownah."

"Yes," she said with a smile. "It is. That's your own private beach. You own it."

"Pahties on the beach," he murmured, directing his comment to no one.

He gazed through the glass for some time, leaving us to wonder about his thoughts. Teddi and I shared a few awkward glances while Vinnie enjoyed the solace that only the ocean could provide. When he was satisfied, he turned to face us.

"Where's the kitchen?" he asked.

"The kitchen is a chef's dream," Teddi said. "Subzero and Wolf appliances. The best of the best."

We toured the kitchen, upstairs, each bedroom, and then walked to the beach. Standing barefoot in the sand, Vinnie faced the home. Fitted with wall-to-wall windows and balconies crafted of the finest stone, the home was breathtaking from the rear.

"Whattabout an offah?" he asked. "Where's the home ownah on offahs?"

"Since the revisions," I said, "we've got two parties

interested at ask. There's nothing solid on the table yet, but we've got—"

He gave me the same wild-eyed glare as when he was stomping Josh's face in. "I fuckin' told ya I wanted to be first one in this fuckin' place, you fuckin' *gidrul*." He looked at Teddi. "What the fuck's wrong with this guy, huh?"

"It wasn't him," Teddi replied, lying even more than me. "It was me. My apologies. I didn't understand your sense of urgency."

"You in chahge?" he asked. "You the ownah of the agency or whatever?"

"I am."

"Whattabout occupancy? When could a person take occupancy?"

"The furniture isn't the owner's. The home is staged," Teddi said. "Occupancy could be immediate. She and her husband have relocated to another local residence. Also, just to be clear, I'm the owner's agent, not yours. I'm looking out for the owner's best interest. Devin, on the other hand, is a neutral party."

"Neutral or not," I said, "it's going to have to be an offer at or above asking price, or I'm—"

He thrust his arms in the air. "Do I look like a fuckin' peasant? You think I'm a fuckin' *gidrul*?"

"Not at all."

He gazed at the back of the home for a moment. "I'll think about." He glanced at his watch. "Tell the *puttana* I'll make an offah tomorrow."

Spanish and Italian were similar in many respects. From my exposure to Hispanics, I knew the word *puttana* translated to *whore*. If he was calling Teddi a whore, he wouldn't be buying the home.

He'd be buying a new set of teeth.

"Who are you talking about?" I asked, trying to squelch my anger. "The *puttana*?"

"The fuckin' home ownah," he replied. "Who else?"

A sense of relief washed over me. Regardless of who Vinnie was or what Teddi stood to gain from his purchase of the home, I couldn't let him speak of her in such a manner. I'd lose my job—and my freedom—to protect her or her image.

"The earlier the better," I said.

"I get up at four thirty," he said. "What time you open?"

"I get there at nine," I said.

He slapped me on the shoulder. "*A domani.*"

★ ★ ★

"I can't take this," Teddi said as she strode past my desk. "I've never been this nervous in my lifetime." She passed in the other direction. "If he doesn't buy the home, I don't know what we're going to do."

"Whatever happens, happens," I said. "If he walks in and sees you pacing the floor, he's going to know he's the only one interested and that we were bullshitting him yesterday. It's just after nine. He'll either call or show up soon, I'm sure of it."

She raked her fingers into the sides of her hair. "What if he doesn't want it?"

"He wants it," I said. "My guess is it's going to be a matter of what the owner's willing to accept. I just hope he doesn't submit a lowball offer."

She blew me a kiss. "I'm going to go vomit."

"Don't forget to brush your teeth afterward," I said with a laugh.

I wanted the home to sell as much as she did. If it didn't,

there wasn't anything I could do to change it. In following my morning routine, I started my playlist and turned the volume to a moderate level. As I scoured the internet for gift ideas, "Sinister Kid" by the Black Keys began. Tapping my fingers to the music, I looked up.

Vinnie's black Cadillac approached the front door at the pace of a crawl. Blocking the sidewalk from any pedestrian traffic, it rolled to a stop.

The passenger door opened. A middle-aged man with the upper body of a deadlifter struggled to fit his body through the door opening. Wearing an old-school zip-up track suit, he looked the part of an Italian triggerman.

The car's trunk popped open.

The musclebound passenger waddled to the trunk, reached inside, and produced a small gym bag. After draping it over his shoulder, he slammed the trunk closed.

While I gazed at the oversized thug with curious eyes, Vinnie got out of the car and stretched. He gestured toward the front of the building. The goombah nodded. Together, they sauntered toward the front door, each of them having the same bravado characteristics to their gait.

The thug opened the door and held it. Vinnie stepped through the opening and did the same thing I did when I saw the entrance for the first time. He gawked at the newly decorated space.

He slapped the meathead's massive bicep. "Talk about *nuotare nell'oro.*"

The tracksuit-wearing thug nodded.

Vinnie met my gaze as he made his way to my desk. "Fuckin' old lady wrecked her Bentley in front of the Dunkin' Donuts. We couldn't get out of there for thirty fuckin' minutes.

Puttana ran the red light. Van hit her, truck hit the van, and one of those fuckin' Mini Coopahs hit the fuckin' truck. *Bam! Bam! Bam!* Just like that. Watched it through the window. Paulie pulled the door open on the Mini Coopah. Girl didn't have a fuckin' scratch on her."

"Sounds like a hell of a wreck," I said.

"Truck had a load of roofing materials. Fuckin' shit's spread from here to that island down south. If anyone's leaving, tell them to take Vanderbilt or be prepared for a fuckin' wait."

I turned down the music and stood. "I'll do it."

"You and me," Vinnie said, leaning against the countertop. "We can talk. Just you and me?"

I had no idea what he was talking about. I nodded anyway. "Absolutely."

"Theoretically speakin', I can buy that house with cash. No?"

For effect, Hollywood movies portrayed a million dollars as being physically larger than it is in real life. In reality, a million dollars in hundred-dollar bills weighed twenty-two pounds and could easily fit into a small backpack, a briefcase, or a gym bag. Nevertheless, sixty million dollars would require a few wheelbarrows, sixty backpacks, or sixty briefcases, and weigh roughly half as much as the Mini Cooper Vinnie was referencing.

I wondered if the gym rat was carrying a down payment in his bag.

"Sure," I said. "We could work out something with cash. What are you thinking?"

"Let's say I have Brunei ten-thousand-dollah notes. They're the same as Singapore notes. The exchange rate is one to one. For the hassle of getting it exchanged to US dollahs,

I'll give the *puttana* the US equivalent of sixty-two million in Brunei dollahs." He cocked his head to the side. "We got a deal?"

My heart raced at the thought of him buying the home, but I had no earthly idea if we could accept that much cash. Hell, I didn't know if we could accept Brunei money at all. I knew that banks typically exchanged foreign currency. In Naples it had to be a common occurrence, considering the foreign population. Sixty million dollars, however, was a little excessive.

"You've got sixty million in cash?" I asked, knowing there was no way he was carrying one-tenth of that much money.

"Sixty-two million," he replied. "In US equivalence." He nodded toward the goombah. "Paulie's got eight thousand four hundred and thirty-two bills in that bag. It's worth sixty-two million in US dollahs at today's exchange rate."

Simple math told me that eighty-four hundred ten-thousand-dollar bills would weigh roughly eighty-four percent of what a million dollars weighed. In short, less than twenty pounds.

"I'm about to piss my pants," I said, lying through my teeth. "I was headed that way when you came in. Can you give me a minute?"

He shrugged. "Sure."

I made a beeline to Teddi's office. Once inside, I shut the door. "You're not going to fucking believe this."

She looked up from her computer monitor. "What?"

"Vinnie's out there with almost eighty-four million and a half Brunei dollars in ten-thousand-dollar notes. He wants to know if we can take—"

"Oh. My. God." She leaped up from her seat. "You're kidding me!"

"I'm serious."

With one hand covering her heart and her eyes as big as saucers, she tugged the hem of her dress down. "Tell him yes."

I was sure she misunderstood. Maybe in my excitement, I didn't convey it properly. My eyes narrowed in opposition. "It's not US currency."

"I heard," she said with a nod. "It's Brunei. BND. It's not as uncommon as you think. They're one of only two countries that make a ten-thousand-dollar note. Singapore and Brunei. They're locked at one to one in exchange. Money launderers use Brunei money all the time. It's easy to hide, travel with, and transport."

"So, I tell him okay?"

"Absolutely." She cleared the edge of the desk and walked toward me. "We'll need to verify the authenticity of the money and count it, of course, but we'll accept it without question." She turned toward her desk. "I don't know what the exchange rate is right now. What's that equate to in US dollars?"

"Sixty-two million," I said.

"Two million over ask?" Her hands shot to her cheeks. "You're kidding?"

"I'm not."

She coughed out a laugh. "Who is this guy?"

Herb told me Vinnie had more money than sense, but in my wildest dreams I wouldn't have imagined something like this ever happening.

"I'm beginning to wonder." I gestured toward the door. "He thinks I'm in the bathroom. Give me, I don't know, five minutes. After that, just wander out there and ask how it's going or something."

"All right, I'll come out in five minutes." She gave me a

kiss. "I can't believe this. I'm so proud of you."

I turned toward the door. "It's not over yet."

Attempting to act indifferent regarding the all-cash transaction, I returned to my desk and let out an exaggerated sigh. "All right, where were we?"

"You were going to ask Bahbie if she could accept Brunei dollahs," he said with a dry laugh. "What'd she say?"

I chuckled. "She said yes."

He slapped his hand against the countertop. "*I contanti, per favore.*"

The goombah dropped the bag onto the counter, unzipped it, and began slapping banded stacks of bills onto the marble surface, side by side. When the stack was so high I could barely peer over the top of it, I shifted my attention from the money to Vinnie.

"Do I want to know where this came from?" I asked with a laugh.

"The money's clean," Vinnie said, seeming irritated that I said anything. "There's one more thing, though."

I doubted his response regarding the cash was completely true. There was a reason he had sixty million dollars in Brunei ten-thousand-dollar notes. I didn't press the issue. If Teddi was okay with the deal, I needed to be, too. I scanned the stacks of bills in disbelief and met his stone-faced gaze.

"What is it?" I asked. "The other thing?"

He tilted his head toward Paulie. "The house goes in Paulie's name."

"I'm not sure if we can—"

He waved the back of his hand at the display of cash. "*O mangiar questa minestra o saltar questa finestra.*"

My brows raised. "Translation?"

He folded his arms over his chest. "Take this soup or jump out the fuckin' window."

I gave him a look of disbelief. "You're saying, *take it or leave it*?"

"We'll take it," Teddi said from behind me.

CHAPTER SIXTEEN

TEDDI

A sense of serenity washed over me. I stretched my arms wide. Like an eagle soaring over a wide open plain, I sailed over the six-lane-wide stretch of pavement without an ounce of worry.

"This is crazy!" I shouted. "We're flying."

Devin cocked his head to the side. "This is about as close as you can get."

In fulfilling my promise to do so, I was on the back of Devin's Harley as we rode along a winding road that connected North Naples to Bonita Springs. We weren't traveling much more than forty miles an hour, but it was enough to give me a sense of what it was like to fly.

The wind enveloped me. The aroma of the summer's flowers tickled my nostrils. The palm trees that lined the sides of the street swooshed past. A crew of landscapers in the distance pruned hedges and replaced withered flowers with new ones. I closed my eyes as the aroma of freshly cut grass filled the air. The sights, sounds, and smells that accompanied a motorcycle ride were more than my mind could come to grips with.

He twisted the throttle and accelerated past a soccer mom in a BMW. The sound from the exhaust echoed off the side of her SUV. As we passed, she stared straight ahead, gripping the steering wheel like her life depended on it.

The tattoos and stern look etched on Devin's face was enough to ward off those who felt they might want to approach as he walked through crowds and past patrons of fine-dining establishments. On the highway, the ear-piercing drone from his motorcycle's exhaust obviously served as a warning to those within earshot that the man with his hands draped over the sky-high handlebars wasn't one to be fucked with.

I felt powerful and protected on the back of his motorcycle. Like I too couldn't be intimidated by the lesser humans who dared to occupy the roads in their cages constructed of steel and glass.

My desire to please Devin had opened my eyes—and my mind—to accepting changes in my life. So far, he hadn't steered me in the wrong direction. I hoped our future together was equally as eye-opening and free of regret as our past had been.

"This is crazy," I said. "I can't believe it took me this long to do this."

He coasted to a stop at a traffic light. "It's the best way I've found to clear my mind."

Over the years, I'd seen many bikers stopped at beaches, bars, and alongside the highway as they passed through Naples on their way to who knows where. The men—like the motorcycles they rode—all differed. Each of them, however, possessed the same look.

One of being content.

In the twenty minutes that we'd traveled on Devin's two-wheeled wonder, I felt that I'd somehow managed to join those men. Although we were separated by time and distance, we now shared the very same experience of obtaining a sense of tranquility that could only be derived from a ride on the open road.

A few minutes later, we parked across the street from Devin's favorite coffee shop. A handful of people were seated outside. Sad that we'd stopped but eager to sit down with Devin and express how much I enjoyed our trip, I relaxed against the seat's backrest and ogled the patrons. Some drank from wineglasses while others sipped their drinks from porcelain coffee cups.

Devin turned off the engine and leaned the motorcycle onto the kickstand. After getting off, he extended his hand to help me do the same. Upon seeing the satisfaction plastered all over my face, he grinned.

"I'm glad you enjoyed it."

I stepped off the motorcycle and into the narrow curb-side parking lane. I realized in doing so that half an hour with an eight-hundred-pound vibrator between my legs had done wonders in stimulating my nether region.

In short, my panties were soaked.

"This is embarrassing." I tugged against the inner thighs of my jeans. "I'm soaking wet."

He pulled me into him and kissed me. He slid his hand into the waist of my jeans. The tip of his finger gently grazed the length of my wetness. I pulled my mouth from his and gave him a dirty look.

"Are you really going to tease me like that?" I asked. "Right here?"

He pushed his finger beyond my wet folds. I sucked an uneven breath. He inserted another. I winced.

"Is that better?" he asked.

I ached for him to finger me into oblivion.

I closed my eyes and bucked my hips, forcing my wet pussy against his hand. He obliged, pushing his fingers deeper until the tips tickled my G-spot. He curled them repeatedly, grazing the hypersensitive flesh with each motion. Euphoria smothered me, stripping me of my ability to resist. With each stroke of his fingers, I grew closer to climax. I was seconds from an earth-shattering orgasm when a car whizzed past, the rush of air in its wake a reminder that we were standing in a public street.

I opened my eyes.

Many of the coffee shop's patrons were unaware I was two finger strokes away from reaching climax, while others seemed all too interested in what we were doing. Being fingered while I stood in the narrow two-lane road wasn't the best of ideas.

I glared, but in a playful way. "You make me mad."

He smirked. "Do I?"

"You're starting something you can't finish," I complained. "So yes, you do."

He pressed his fingertips into my G-spot. "Why can't I finish it?"

"We're standing in the street," I whispered, my body shuddering as I spoke. I nodded toward the patio in the distance. "And there are people over there. A few of them are watching us."

He cocked his head to the side. "Do I look like I give a fuck?"

He didn't. As satisfied as he was with his existence on earth, I doubted he cared what anyone thought of him, including the two women behind him who were now nodding in our direction.

"No," I replied. "You don't."

He studied my face. His eyes narrowed. Using the two fingers that were still buried deep in my throbbing pussy as leverage, he pulled me close to his chest.

"If I want to finger you in the street," he said sternly, "I'll finger you in the street."

"Umm." I swallowed a ball of apprehension. "Okay."

As the two women in the distance watched eagerly, he proceeded to do just that. Seconds later, I was backed against his motorcycle with my eyes rolled back into my head and him leaning over me.

The world around me vanished momentarily, leaving me to enjoy the fruits of Devin's labor in the solace of silence.

My eyes shot open as he brought me to climax. I bit into my lower lip in hopes of stifling my urge to scream out in pleasure. Wondering just what he'd done to change me from the woman who once worried what someone might think about the color of my shoes to one who obviously didn't care if someone watched me being finger-banged while my ass rested against a dusty Harley-Davidson, I looked at Devin, thinking the answer might be hidden somewhere deep in his brown orbs.

His eyes glistened with satisfaction. He curled the tips of his fingers against my G-spot once again for good measure. "You're fucking gorgeous."

I collapsed against his motorcycle, nearly tipping it over. "What . . . what are you doing to me?" I stammered.

He slid his hand from inside my jeans. "Whatever I want to."

That much was obvious. I braced myself against the teetering motorcycle. "I can see that."

"C'mon," he said, tilting his head toward the coffee shop behind him. "Let's go get a cup of coffee."

I situated things the best I could and checked myself in

the motorcycle's rearview mirror. "I look like hell."

"You look fantastic." He draped his left arm over my shoulder. "You always look fantastic."

I tugged my panties out of my crotch and adjusted my ponytail. "I'll take your word for it."

We sauntered across the street. As we strolled past the table where two of the interested parties were seated, Devin paused and faced them. He raised his right hand to his mouth and sucked my juices from the two fingers he'd used to please me.

"Good morning." He lowered his hand and gave the two women a sharp nod. "Beautiful day, isn't it?"

Either incapable of responding or unwilling to do so, they both gawked at us as if we were aliens.

Devin reached for the door and opened it. "After you," he said, gesturing inside.

I stepped into the coffee shop, wearing a prideful smile. There was no doubt Devin was opening my eyes to accepting changes, many of which were in complete contrast to my mundane past. Nevertheless, I had not one single regret.

I hoped that didn't change anytime soon.

CHAPTER SEVENTEEN

DEVIN

Midway through his meatloaf dinner, Herb paused to listen to the newscast playing in the adjoining room. When the segment finished, he shifted his eyes from the television to me.

"Some lady cop posing as a masseuse offered him a hand job. Then she arrested him when he tried to pay her." He waved his fork toward the television. "Did you see that?"

I'd seen the report several times prior. The man, a rich celebrity of sorts, had driven from a wealthy neighborhood in Palm Beach to a seedy massage parlor in a neighboring city.

"Somebody with that much money wouldn't drive from Palm Beach to Jupiter to get a massage unless he wasn't looking for a little something extra," I replied. "I'm guessing he didn't stumble in there by chance."

He pressed the tines of his fork through the corner of his meatloaf and paused. "Man's a billionaire, isn't he?"

"I think so."

"What's a billionaire doing getting hand jobs at a shitty massage parlor, anyway?" he asked.

"That's exactly what I was wondering."

He poked at his food. "What's a hand job cost at a place like that?"

I'd never had a hand job. Considering all the available

options for arousal to the point of ejaculation, a hand job was the clear loser in my opinion.

"Hell, I don't know," I replied. "Twenty bucks?"

"I paid three bucks for one in Da Nang in nineteen sixty-nine," he said. "She yanked on that fucker like she was trying to start a goddamned lawn mower. Each time she tugged on it, I came up off the bed about six inches. I finally told her to stop. Gave her another three bucks for a blowjob. She wanted five, but I talked her down. Felt like I'd cheated her afterward, so I gave her a five-dollar tip. Considering that was fifty years ago in Vietnam, I'm thinking a hand job will go for fifty, here in the States. Maybe more."

"Fifty?" I stared in complete disbelief. "Who'd give fifty bucks for a hand job?"

He nodded toward the living room. "People like him."

"A hand job's worth fifteen bucks and five for the tip," I said. "Twenty total."

He considered my reasoning. He shook his head in opposition. "I bet twenty bucks would buy about three strokes."

"Three strokes?" I couldn't help but laugh. "That's seven bucks a stroke. Applying that math, the fifty-buck hand job you're talking about would buy seven strokes. A girl would have to be pretty talented to finish a guy off in seven strokes."

"Bet that gal you're seeing could get it done in seven strokes, can't she?"

"I don't know," I replied. "She's never given me a hand job."

His fork fell from his grasp and hit his plate with a *clank!* "What?" He seemed appalled. "Why in the hell not?"

"Who wants a hand job?"

He reached for the fallen utensil. "Who doesn't?"

I shrugged and commenced eating my dinner. "I don't."

His wrinkled brow furrowed even more. "Why not?"

"They're dumb," I said over a mouthful of food. "I've got a hell of a lot of options to relieve myself. A hand job is my last choice."

He leaned forward, hovering over his plate, his brows raised in wonder. "Does she give blowjobs?"

"She sure does."

He relaxed into the back in his chair and whistled through his teeth. "Who in their right mind would want a hand job if that was an option?"

I chuckled. "Precisely."

"Does she have you finish on a tissue, or does she collect it in her hand? Midge used a tissue." He shook his head, as if recalling one of their sexual activities together. "Drove me nuts. She always had her left hand dangling at her side clutching a Kleenex. Made it hard for me to stay focused."

I chuckled again. "Neither."

He seemed confused. "What's she do with it?"

"She swallows it."

"Jesus jumped-up Christ," he blurted. He straightened his posture and clapped his hands together. "That gal's a keeper."

"Because she swallows my spunk?"

He raised his index finger. "She's motivated." He raised his middle finger. "Devoted to her job." He continued extending his fingers with each point he made. "Financially stable. Gorgeous. She's got a nice rack. She's got a great personality. And she's willing to do what she must to keep you happy."

She might have taken a ride on my motorcycle, but that

didn't make her willing to do whatever it took to make me happy.

"I'd agree with all of them except for the last one," I said. "It has yet to be seen."

He looked at me like I was crazy. "There's not a girl on this planet who sits in front of the television at night thinking to herself, *damn, I wish I had a mouthful of come.* If they sold that shit in stores, nobody would buy it, even if they set it right beside the Coca-Cola. If restaurants offered it by the glass, nobody'd order it, either." He shook his head as if disgusted with me. "That shit's nasty, and you know it. If she swallows it, she's doing it for no other reason than to keep you happy."

I'd taken her willingness to swallow my load for granted. He had a good point. I doubted anyone yearned for a mouthful of come.

"You're probably right," I said in agreement.

"If she can choke down a mouthful of that shit without complaining, that damned woman's willing to go out of her way to please you," he said, seeming upset that he had to mention it again. "Women like her are few and far between. Understand that. A woman's desire to please a man is worth a lot more than looks or money, that's for damned sure."

"So, I should keep her because she swallows my come?" I asked, my tone coated in sarcasm.

"No," he snapped back. "You keep her for all the reasons I gave you a minute ago, one of which is that she's willing to do whatever it takes to keep you happy." He picked up his plate and stood. He gave me a flippant look. "You might be intelligent, but you're slowly proving that common sense isn't something you possess."

"Fuck you, old man."

"I made my point." He turned toward the kitchen. "Now you need to prove your worth by being man enough keep her."

I had no immediate plans to get rid of her. If nothing changed, I could see us staying together until I was free to decide where I chose to call home.

"I'll probably keep her around until I'm free to go to the other side of the state," I said. "Then I guess we'll see what happens. I doubt she's up for a move to Miami."

"Miami?" He tossed his plate into the sink. "There ain't one of those pricks you used to run with who gives an honest fuck about you. Your best bet is to make a change with who you run with."

"They're a good bunch of guys," I said. "They really are."

Now facing me, his disapproval of my claim was apparent. He looked like he just swallowed a cat turd.

"Are they?" He put his hands on his hips. "How many of 'em came to visit you in the joint?"

"Bikers aren't much for visiting prisons," I replied.

"How many of 'em wrote you letters?"

The only person who wrote me while I was locked up was Herb. I'd looked forward to his letters as much as I'd anticipated the arrival of Christmas as a child. Without them, I would have had no connection to the outside world.

"I'll take that dumb look on your face as a response that none of them did," he quipped. "Any of 'em send you a few bucks for snacks?"

They hadn't, but I hadn't expected them to, either.

He coughed a dry laugh. "That's what I thought." He turned toward the living room. "You're like that Ferrari that's always parked down at that crappy car dealer on Pine Ridge. Your presence elevates their worth. They keep you around because it makes them look good. Rest assured, none of those worthless bastards will be at your side when you're drawing your last dying breath."

I felt the need to rebut his statement, but I couldn't. As much as I didn't like hearing them, the points he made were all valid.

None of them, however, were what I wanted to hear.

CHAPTER EIGHTEEN

TEDDI

Seated beside me on the couch, Devin held his phone at arm's length. He gave me an apologetic look. When the voice on the other end went silent, he raised it to his ear. "I'm not going to do anything stupid. You can stop calling. Everything's fine."

Having Devin stay in my home was a huge step for me, even if it was only for one night. My life's sexual encounters hadn't been infrequent by anyone's standards, but I had a rule I followed with each man I slept with.

I didn't bring them into my home.

The exceptions were the two long-term relationships I'd been in. Having both of them end poorly supported my belief that allowing men into my home was a precursor to a relationship's failure.

I hoped that this time things were different.

"Fine," Devin said, his voice thick with frustration. "I'll call you in the morning."

He hung up the phone. He tossed it to the far end of the couch and shook his head. "That old man drives me nuts."

"I think it's cute that he cares enough to call."

"Three times?" Devin asked. "Since we got off work?"

"What do you two normally do on Friday night?"

"Same thing we do every night. Watch *Wheel of Fortune*

and *Jeopardy*. Talk about whatever is in the news. Get into an argument about our differing opinions. I go to the gym at the clubhouse and work out, and he goes to bed. Same thing every night."

"He probably misses you."

"I'm sure he does," he said. "But I'm not going to live with him forever."

A tinge of hope ran through me. But I feared asking where he intended to move would produce an answer I didn't want to hear.

"How long has it been since his wife passed?" I asked.

"I don't know. Ten years, maybe?"

"I'm sure he looks forward to your company. This is the first night you've been away, isn't it?"

"Since I moved in? Yeah."

Being in a relationship required maintenance, part of which was provided—to me at least—in the form of advice from friends who had been through the same experiences. I wondered if Devin relied on Herb for advice, or if Kate was his go-to sounding board.

"What do you guys talk about every night?" I asked.

"Dumb shit." He chuckled and then looked at me. "What's a hand job worth?"

I gave him a look. "A what?"

"Hand job," he said. "You know. Giving a guy a handy."

I repositioned myself to face him. "Jacking someone off?"

"Yeah."

"What's it worth? Like what should a prostitute charge?"

"Someone in a massage parlor," he replied. "How much extra should it cost for a hand job? On top of the massage price. This was our topic of discussion last week."

"What's a massage cost?" I asked.

"Hundred bucks." He shrugged. "Give or take."

I'd given a plethora of hand jobs in my days, but I wouldn't jack off a random guy for any amount of money. If a massage therapist's menu included hand jobs, I suspected they'd be priced affordably and within reach of his or her clientele.

"I don't know," I replied. "Two hundred bucks?"

"Two hundred bucks?" He looked at me up and down. "For a hand job?"

I'd lived a somewhat sheltered life. Feeling foolish for my response, I scrunched my nose in dramatic fashion. "Is that too much?"

"I'm guessing for two hundred bucks you could have sex with half the staff."

"Really?"

"It can't cost more than a hundred for sex," he replied. "I'm not speaking from experience. That's just a guess. I bet it's accurate, though."

I couldn't claim that I'd never had meaningless sex. I could, however, state that I'd never had sex for money. I saw the two as being completely different. Being a prostitute required a woman to have sex with anyone who could afford to pay for it. Having meaningless sex with a random barfly allowed the woman to choose her partner.

"That's gross," I said.

He chuckled. "Which part of it?"

"That someone would have sex for a hundred bucks."

"What if they charged a thousand?" he asked. "Does that make it classy?"

"No," I replied. "It's still gross."

"What about the hand job? Is that gross, too?"

In high school, I viewed sex as a sacred act. Consequently, I doled out hand jobs to my male classmates like ammunition to a deployed brigade of US Marines.

"Jacking someone off is different," I replied. "It's not sex."

"What is it?"

"I don't know. It's a hand job."

He laughed. "You act like you're experienced."

"I've given a few," I said.

"Define *a few*."

We'd agreed to be transparent with one another. As much as I hated to admit the truth, I felt I had to. With some reluctance, I responded in a less than definitive manner.

"In high school, I didn't have sex. With anyone. So, I gave hand jobs."

He laughed. "Two-hundred-dollar hand jobs?"

"What?" I blurted. "No."

"Earlier, you said a hand job should be worth two hundred bucks. Were yours worth two hundred?"

"I never had any complaints," I replied, reflecting more pride in my response than I probably should have.

"I've never had a hand job."

There was no way he'd gone a lifetime without being jacked off a few times by nervous high school girls who were saving their virginity for marriage. I suspected what he meant was that he never had a hand job worth mentioning. I wanted to hear the sordid details surrounding his haphazard hand jobs.

"You've never had a good one?" I asked.

"I've never had one, period." He unzipped his pants and pulled out his cock. "Let's see what you've got."

I alternated eager glances between his dick and his eyes.

"You've never had a hand job? Not even a bad one?"

"No." He calmly stroked his cock. "I haven't."

I pried my eyes away from his cock-filled hand. "Why?"

"Hand jobs are stupid," he replied. "I'm pretty sure I wouldn't even come."

"Can I try?" I asked excitedly.

"Well," he said with a laugh, "I didn't get it out so *I* could play with it."

A tinge of anxiety tickled my senses. Enthusiasm promptly replaced it. I sprang from my seat. "I'll be right back."

I ran to my bathroom and grabbed my lotion from the vanity. I had no doubt that I'd be a little rusty after two decades of hand job inactivity, but a bone-dry tug job would place me in a category where I clearly didn't belong.

Nina Hartman might have been the homecoming queen of Gulf Coast High, but I was the unnamed hand job queen. I fully intended to prove it to a man who appeared to doubt my worth.

Lotion in hand, I returned to the living room. Hoping to dispel the myth that hand jobs were stupid, I sat cross-legged on the floor in front of him. "Jeans and boxers off, mister."

"Oh. Wow. You're serious."

"That's right."

He rid himself of his boots, jeans, and boxers. As if it were an everyday occurrence, he took his seat and continued stroking himself.

"Are you ready?" I asked.

With his thick shaft clenched in his fist, he gazed at me with eyes of uncertainty. "Are you?"

I pumped a few squirts of lotion into my palm and met his doubtful gaze. I reached for his cock. "I am now."

"Want to make a bet?" he asked.

I stroked his shaft once. "What kind of bet?"

"Whether or not you can make me come."

"What's the wager?"

"The winner gets sex on command from the loser."

He had my full attention. I swallowed heavily. "On command?"

"Yep."

If he won, he'd probably demand that I fuck him in my office or in the front seat of my Range Rover at some busy intersection. If I won, I'd come up with something far more interesting.

"I'll take that bet," I said with a nod of reassurance.

He playfully wagged his cock at me. "Get to work. Let me know when your arm's too tired to continue. I'll finish it off."

I looked at him and smirked. "Just relax. This will be over before you know it."

I stroked his shaft from the tip to the base a few times and then paused. "Are you opposed to standing?"

"Whatever you think might give you the edge," he said with a light laugh. "But it's not going to work."

I inched away from the couch and removed my shirt and bra. I cupped my boobs in my hand and gave him an innocent look. "When you come, would you do it on my boobs?"

He stood. "You're not going to have to worry about that."

"Don't be so sure of yourself, mister." I gestured to his shirt. "Toss the shirt too, boss."

He removed his shirt and added it to the pile. His midsection was chiseled to perfection. The washboard of muscles covered in tattooed skin tapered to a prominent V. Beneath it, a gorgeous cock that was arrow straight and as thick as my dainty wrist.

His body, in its entirety, demanded admiration. It begged to be touched. I knelt in front of him and traced my fingers over the ripples of muscle that separated his chest from the object of my current desires.

I reached for his cock. "Prepare to be defeated."

He crossed his arms over his tattooed chest and glared.

I fixed my eyes on the prize and stroked his entire length with a firm—but gentle—grip. Hoping for reassurance that my efforts were pleasing him, I glanced up.

He peered at me with disbelieving eyes. "I don't think being jacked off is my thing."

I wasn't about to forfeit my crown. I cupped his balls in my left hand and shortened my stroke. Paying special attention to the rim of the head, I stroked his stiff dick like I was jackhammering through construction rubble—all the while holding his doubtful gaze.

I parted my lips slightly. "Come in my mouth," I cooed. "Or on my face." I tossed my hair over my shoulders and gave him my best sultry look. "Just cover me in it. Please."

The doubt in his eyes faded to nothing. Eager to win the bet, I continued my firm-gripped onslaught, maintaining a methodical pace. I daydreamed of the places that I might command him to have sex with me. The sound of his irregular breathing brought me from my dreamlike state.

His eyes widened. His back arched. The worried look on his face gave indication that he was seconds away from losing his composure—and the bet. A few strokes later, his cock swelled in my hand.

With my mouth agape and tits at the ready, I stroked his thick shaft vigorously. Hoping nothing came between me and success, I mentally prepared for him to release his pleasure, wondering just how much a man like him would discharge.

If masculinity had anything to do with it, he'd unload a quart. If sexiness were involved, it'd be a gallon. If the size of his cock or balls came into play, it would take me an hour to clean up.

He didn't make me wonder for long. The only forewarning to his climactic finish was the long, guttural groan that escaped from deep within his being.

His eyes cinched closed.

Come blasted from the tip of his cock like a geyser. In a nanosecond, my face and tits were covered in my successes.

Many women would perceive the event as tasteless.

Gross.

Nasty.

I saw it as nothing short of a sexy-as-absolute-fuck success. Devin was a man's man. He'd never received a hand job and doubted I'd be able to succeed in pleasing him. So certain of my inability, he'd made a bet against me bringing him to climax.

Despite his disbeliefs, I'd accomplished my goal. The depth of his pleasure was plastered all over my face and tits.

With an elevated sense of self-worth, I cupped my come-drenched breasts in my hands and stood. Devin's eyes were now open and wider than I'd ever seen them.

"I'm going to clean this off," I said.

Wearing a grin, I strode toward the bathroom as proud as a peacock. Upon reaching the door, I paused and glanced over my shoulder. "Don't forget," I said. "It's sex *on command*."

He exhaled a long, exaggerated breath. "Got any ideas?"

When he found out what I wanted from him, he'd probably forfeit the bet. If not, we'd both have an unbelievable story to tell when it was over.

"Not yet," I lied. "I'll have to think about it."

CHAPTER NINETEEN

DEVIN

Kate ran through the front door, narrowly escaping the torrential downpour that swept across the parking lot. Appearing relieved that her new hairstyle was spared, she came to my desk and let out a sigh.

Her normally wavy hair was now arrow straight. The few golden highlights she wore had been tastefully increased to give her hair a summery glow without looking fake or unnatural.

"I like the new hair," I said. "The highlights look great."

"Thank you." She flipped the straightened strands over her shoulder and struck a pose as if modeling for a magazine cover. "Simple Beauty Studio nailed it. It's called twilighting."

"Whatever it's called, they did a great job," I said in agreement.

"Enough about the awesome job they did on my hair." She leaned against the edge of my desk and raised her perfectly sculpted brows. "Sounds like you and Teddi are getting ready for an exciting night."

Apparently she knew something I didn't. It wasn't surprising. It seemed Kate and Teddi talked as much as Herb and me.

"What are you talking about?" I asked.

She rested her chin against the heel of her palm. "Sex. On. Demand."

Prior to being surrounded by women on a daily basis, I had no idea they spoke to one another about sex. Unlike men, I assumed they kept their tales to themselves, leaving each other to wonder what they were doing, who they were seeing, and how frequently they were being screwed by their respective other.

I narrowed my gaze. "She told you about that?"

"She tells me everything."

I swallowed hard. "Everything?"

She wagged her eyebrows. "Everything."

"You might think she tells you everything, but—"

"You lasted all of thirty seconds," she said, straight-faced. "It took her longer to clean up the mess than it did for her to bring you to climax."

Slightly embarrassed, I felt the need to defend myself the best I was able. "She used lotion," I complained. "Did she tell you that?"

Her gaze narrowed. "What does that have to do with anything?"

"It was some super-slippery secret stash she kept hidden in the bathroom. It gave her a competitive edge."

"You think she used lotion for a competitive edge?" She looked at me like I was an idiot. "That's basic hand job etiquette."

"How the hell am I supposed to know that?" I snapped back. "I'm not versed in the intricacies of hand job delivery."

"Well, now you know," she said. "Using lotion is standard operating procedure for a hand job."

"What if it's a hand job emergency?" I asked.

She scrunched her nose. "What's a hand job emergency?"

"An impromptu thing. Say, if the guy was driving down the street and you felt like it was a perfect time to jack him off. What then?"

"We keep it in our purse," she replied, as if it were common knowledge.

Once again, it appeared I was the idiot. "You keep jack-off juice in your purse?"

She nodded. "We carry lotion with us in case we're challenged by a nonbeliever to stroke him to climactic bliss."

"Are you serious?" I asked.

"Absolutely," she said with a nod. "We're inundated with requests to jack guys off. We need lotion to minimize friction and guarantee success. Until now, it's been a well-kept secret. You figured us out."

I had no idea if she was serious or joking. She looked serious.

"Seriously?"

"It's a huge conspiracy," she admitted. "To tell you the truth, I don't think I'm supposed to let you know these types of things. It goes against girl code."

I knew women were sneaky bitches, but I had no idea they'd banded together to develop a recipe of success for jacking men off. I wondered what else I needed to prepare for.

"What other tricks do you sneaky fuckers have up your sleeves?" I asked.

She took a few steps away from the desk. "I probably shouldn't say."

"We're best friends," I pleaded. "C'mon."

She looked me over as if sizing me up for a suit. "Well, since we're besties." She glanced over each shoulder. Upon realizing there was no one within earshot, she came closer. "If you ever do anything stupid like stay out late with your friends and get shitfaced, and you want a quick way to be forgiven? All you've got to do is go downtown. But it's got to be a solo effort. No reciprocal action."

"You mean…" I stuck my tongue between the V of my outstretched index and middle finger. "This?"

"You guessed it."

"Solo effort, huh?"

She nodded. "All will be forgiven."

"What else?"

"Every chance you get, walk around the house shirtless. It stimulates our sexual senses."

"That's an easy one," I said. "Keep 'em coming."

"No matter how cool you think it would be or how much you might think she'd like it, never ask for a three-way. It's the kiss of death to any relationship."

"I'd never ask anyone to—"

"Just making sure."

"What else?"

"No matter what the food we cook tastes like, tell us you love it. Rave about it. Compare it to a recent fine-dining experience. It's a surefire way to get post-meal sex."

"Anything else?"

She smirked. "I think that's it for now."

"What?" I asked. "There's something you don't want to tell me."

"Well…" She gave me a quick once-over. "No. Forget it."

I scowled. "Say what you were going to say."

Seeming reluctant to continue, she turned away. "Just go with what I gave you."

"Bullshit," I spat. "Tell me what you were going to say."

"Fine." She faced me and let out a sigh. "At that instant our vaginal walls tighten up, just before an orgasm, we love having a finger poked up our butt."

"No shit?"

"I'm dead serious. It's a well-guarded secret. Make sure your nails are trimmed. And be sure to lick it first if there's no lube available. But do it in secrecy. Don't advertise that you're doing it. It's the surprise that excites us."

"I'll keep that in mind." I extended my hand and clenched my fist. "Appreciate it."

"No problem, bro." She pounded her fist against mine. "Just keep it a secret."

I pinched my fingers together and zipped my lips closed.

She turned toward her office. "Have fun this weekend."

"What's going on this weekend?"

She disappeared into the office's abyss, leaving me to wonder what Teddi's plans were for the weekend.

Some secrets, I guessed, were meant to be kept.

CHAPTER TWENTY

TEDDI

Devin took a sip of his wine and set the glass aside. He reached for his fork. "This is crazy."

The only thing that was crazy was that he was eating dinner without his shirt. It was hard for me to stay focused on my meal, and I feared that I might be caught inadvertently drooling.

"What's crazy?" I asked, assuming he wasn't talking about his bare torso.

"This lasagna," he replied. "It's better than what Herb and I ate that night we met Vinnie at that fancy Italian joint."

I shifted my eyes from my food to him. "You like it?"

"It's awesome," he said. "The salad, too. The dressing is fantastic."

The muscles in his chest swelled with each breath he took, and he took them often. I felt like I did in ninth grade when Karen Valentine and I peered through the crack in the wall and into the boys' locker room. I wanted to stare but felt guilty for doing so.

I shifted my attention to my plate. "It's just oil and vinegar."

"Well, whatever it is, it's fucking tasty."

Despite my intentions to stay focused on the meal, I

glanced in his direction. He raised a forkful of lasagna to his mouth. Whether intentional or not, his pectoral muscle flexed. Then it flexed again.

I nearly wet myself.

"Thank you," I murmured, looking away. "I appreciate it."

"So, what movie are we going to see?"

"*Ford versus Ferrari*," I replied. "There's not a good rom-com playing, so I thought we'd do a guy show." I made the mistake of looking up. "They say it's really good."

"Sounds good to me." He nodded toward the island. "Can I have some more before we go?"

"Salad?"

"Everything," he said. "Salad. Lasagna. The bread. I can't get enough."

We were eating later than I'd hoped and were pressed for time, but I beamed with pride at the thought of him enjoying the meal. "Absolutely." I stood and reached over the table. "Hand me your plate."

He lifted his plate and extended his arm over the table. The muscles on the back of his bicep flared to twice their normal size. His shirtless antics had me so horny, I was lightheaded. Itching to get my plan underway, I took his plate and filled it with food. After a moment of admiring him from my out-of-view vantage point, I returned to the table.

I handed him the plate. "I just noticed you're half naked. What's going on with that?"

"I didn't want to wrinkle that new shirt you bought me," he said. "I thought it'd be nice to wear it out."

"I think that's a great idea," I said. "If we're not taking the motorcycle, I'll wear a dress."

If I drove, it would make succeeding that much easier.

I finished my meal and excused myself from the table while my shirtless boyfriend continued to shovel food into his gullet like a starving man.

"I'm going to get dressed really quickly," I said, glancing at my watch as I stood. "We need to leave in thirty minutes or so."

"I'll be ready."

"Okay."

I changed into my evening's attire of a comfortable dress, two-inch heels, and my favorite accessories. After primping my hair to perfection, I returned to the kitchen. Although the dinner mess was cleaned up, Devin remained shirtless and was pacing the floor.

"Are you about ready?" I asked.

He paused. "Just about."

He kissed me—passionately. As he broke our embrace, he lifted me from my feet.

Lightheaded from the kiss, I mentally fumbled to figure out what was happening. "What are you doing?"

He lowered my butt onto the edge of the island. "Sorry I was late."

"That's okay," I said. "We've still got time."

He glanced at his watch. "About five more minutes?"

I looked at the clock on the microwave. "Give or take. Why?"

He pushed my dress to mid-thigh. "Get this thing out of my way."

Confused, I gave him a look. "What are we doing?"

"I'm going to lick your pussy for five minutes," he replied. "Until we've got to go."

Licking my pussy trumped a movie about men racing

cars. We could be an hour late for all I cared. As luck would have it, I was sans panties. Eager to let him get to work, I hiked my dress to my waist and spread my legs so wide, I feared I might dislocate a hip.

"How's that?" I asked.

He wedged his shoulders between my thighs and lowered his head into my lap. "Perfect."

I rested my elbows against the island. I peered down at him. His warm breath against my wet pussy caused me to shake with anticipation.

He flicked his tongue against my clit. My body shuddered. He did it again. He slid a finger inside me. A few gentle strokes followed. He added another finger.

He gripped my ass firmly in his hands and pressed his mouth against my throbbing pussy. I bucked my hips against his face, maintaining perfect timing with flicks of his tongue.

Flick, flick, suck.

Flick, flick, suck.

Flick, flick, suck.

The man was focused. His determination was undeniable. I shook like a silenced cell phone as he continued to tongue his way into my heart.

My body tensed. I pawed at the cold marble surface. Nearly frantic, I reached for his head. After receiving no opposition, I began fucking his mouth. He responded by sucking my clit like a man who'd received formal training on the subject.

Seconds later, a paralyzing orgasm rendered me incapable of doing anything but mindlessly staring at the ceiling while I climaxed all over his freshly shaven face.

A hint of Devin's cologne, fresh garlic, and the aroma

of sex melded together. The combined scents, the earth-shattering orgasm, and my eager anticipation of the night's future events turned my brain to mush.

He kissed my inner thighs and then stood.

I tilted my head to the side.

Wearing a smirk, he met my glassy-eyed gaze. He wiped his mouth on the back of his hand. "You ready to go?"

He'd sucked me stupid. I doubted I could remember how to walk, let alone drive. Nevertheless, forfeiting my plans for the night wasn't an option.

"If you're ready to carry me," I said, "I'm ready to go."

★ ★ ★

We took our assigned seats in the front of the theater, three rows from the screen. Devin surveyed the handful of empty seats behind us and then looked at me.

"Why the fuck are we sitting way up here?" he whispered. "There are a few seats back there."

"When I looked online, it showed all those as sold."

"Rich bastards in this town buy all these seats and then never show up," he complained. "I swear."

"These seats will be fine," I whispered.

We sat side by side in the center of the aisle. The three narrow rows of seats were three steps down the stairway from the much wider rows behind us. Segregated from the rest of the moviegoers at a movie that was beginning to lose its lure, we had our own private section, of sorts.

Following the previews, the movie began. A few scenes into the show, a foul-mouthed British man was racing against many other similar cars on a racetrack that appeared to be in the desert. Everyone in attendance, including Devin, had their eyes glued to the screen. My interest wasn't in the movie, nor would it be.

I tapped my finger against Devin's thigh.

He glanced at me. His eyes quickly shot back to the racing scene. "What?" he asked over the sound of the speeding cars.

"Take off your pants," I said. "And your boxers."

He gave me a look. "What the fuck for?"

"Sex on demand," I replied, trying not to smile.

His eyes darted to the massive screen. He chuckled.

"I'm serious," I said. "You lost the bet. I'm demanding it."

He glanced behind him. "There's a hundred people back there." He looked at me. "A hundred people with an average age of seventy."

"On demand," I said, wagging my finger toward his crotch. "Take 'em off."

He studied me for a long moment before complying with my request. He mumbled protests under his breath as he removed each article of clothing.

Uncertain if his complaining was driven by a reluctance to perform in front of a theater full of elderly onlookers or the fact that he was going to miss a good part of the movie, I offered a less than heartfelt apology.

"We can come back and see the movie later," I whispered. "But this is happening, boss."

"Just remember," he said, tossing his boxer shorts into the empty seat at his side. "You asked for it."

I gripped his semi-flaccid cock in my hand and gave it a few strokes. "Are you going to be able to perform, or am I going to have to make do with this noodle?"

"It's hard to focus," he complained. "There's a lot going

on in here." He nodded toward my purse. "You got any lotion in there?"

"I don't need lotion," I replied in braggadocian fashion.

I buried my face in his lap and sucked him into a rock-hard state. Satisfied that we were both prepped and ready, I raised my head and wiped my mouth on the back of my hand. I surveyed the theater. All eyes appeared to be fixed on the movie.

Facing the screen, I climbed on Devin's lap and lowered myself onto his stiff dick. Once his length was buried deep inside me, I glanced over my shoulder.

"I'm going to ride you like a stolen bike," I bragged.

I gripped the back of the seat in front of me and braced myself. I gyrated my hips with the timing and precision of a dancer. Working my pussy up and down the full length of Devin's rigid shaft, I took deliberate strokes. It was the first time we'd had sex that I was in charge of the operation.

It felt magnificent.

If it was the excitement of having sex in a full theater or that I was riding him in my favorite position, I didn't know, but sixty seconds into the act, I was on the verge of a sexual meltdown. I slowed my pace, but it provided little relief from the euphoria that was building within me.

I accepted my sexual fate and continued at a predictable pace. Just this once it was going to be about me, not Devin. I didn't care if I needed to give him a hand job when I was done, I fully intended to get what was rightfully mine without apology, explanation, or reservation.

Four carefully timed strokes later, the end was imminent. Knowing the next stroke would certainly be my last, I drew a shallow breath. I slowly lowered myself the length of his shaft.

As each swollen inch of his girth penetrated me, my vaginal walls contracted a little more.

At the instant the tip of his dick pressed against my cervix, my pussy clenched his swollen cock like a vise. As I relished in the orgasm that began to take possession of my very being, Devin's finger found its way into my ass.

I hadn't expected it, nor was it something I would have asked for in my wildest dreams. Nevertheless, the insertion of that single digit not only took me by surprise, but it also sent me through the climactic roof like a Saturn-bound sex rocket.

Incapable of suppressing my pleasure, I wailed out my satisfaction in the form of a blood-curdling carnal scream. At the same instant, the scene on the screen changed from a hundred-decibel auto race to a quiet office setting.

If the people in attendance weren't aware of what we were doing prior to my outburst, they were afterward. Claiming it was anything other than sexual wasn't a remote possibility. Embarrassed, exhausted, and satisfied beyond words, I hid between Devin and the seat in front of him.

"Jesus, Teddi," he complained. "Make it obvious."

I withered into his lap. "Sorry."

I took my seat and watched the remainder of the two-and-a-half-hour-long movie. When it ended, we waited for the theater to empty and then rose from our seats.

I strutted out of the theater at Devin's side. Once in the corridor, I gestured toward the bathrooms.

"I need to use the restroom."

He kissed me. "Me too."

Once inside, I glanced in the mirror. I looked like one of the many drunken celebrity mugshots that often circulated through social media circles. My dress was wrinkled, my hair resembled the Bride of Frankenstein's, and my makeup was smeared beyond repair.

After ten minutes of primping, I felt that I was presentable enough to sneak out of the theater, hopefully unnoticed. Proud of my movie theater accomplishment but frustrated with my disheveled appearance, I meandered out of the bathroom with my shoulders slumped.

Devin was in the corridor, talking to a well-dressed elderly man. A very familiar well-dressed elderly man that I didn't want to recognize me.

I lowered my head and turned toward the exit. "Let's go," I murmured.

"Hold up a minute," Devin said. "I want you to meet someone."

Fuck. Fuck. Fuckity-fuck.

I turned to face them. As I made eye contact with the suit-wearing billionaire, I feigned surprise. "Harry Morgan?"

He alternated glances between Devin and me and then met my reluctant gaze. "Teddi Mack?"

I stepped in front of him and shook his hand. "How are you doing, Harry?"

He smirked. "Not as good as you, I suppose."

I suspected he'd heard of the sale of Margaret's beachfront mansion. "Oh? Why do you say that?"

He glanced at Devin and then at me. The corners of his mouth curled up slightly. "You two were in the front row of the theater, weren't you?"

My face flushed red hot. "We were."

"I've been trying to talk Maggie into something like that for a lifetime," Harry said with a laugh. "She's far too prudent to agree to it, though."

I didn't know what to say. I offered him a crumpled smile.

Following a moment of awkward silence, he gave a crisp nod. "Nice to see you again, Teddi."

"Nice to see you, too," I replied.

Devin shook his hand. "I'll look forward to your call."

He patted Devin's shoulder. "Enjoy your youth."

Devin draped his arm over my shoulder. Red-faced and embarrassed beyond words, I shuffled toward the door.

"He wants to sell his house," Devin said. "There's one in Port Royal he's got his eye on. He said it's time to downsize."

Harry's home was one of Naples's most prestigious. To date, it was the most expensive piece of real estate I'd ever sold.

I raised my head. "Really?"

"We were talking about the movie, and he commented about the 'people up front who were having fun.' I laughed like I had no idea who they were, and the conversation went to my tattoos. Then he asked, 'Where's a guy like you get a job?' But he said it jokingly. I told him where I worked, and he said, 'I know a gal who works there. She sold me the house I'm living in. I was planning on giving her a call.' Then you walked out of the bathroom. It was like a lightbulb went off when he realized we were the two in the front of the theater."

"Perfect," I said in a sarcastic tone. "Just perfect. I can't believe he saw us doing that."

He paused. "I can't take these tattoos on and off. I like it that way. It forces me to be the same guy whether I'm at work, a biker rally, or a movie theater. I can't fake my way into being anyone other than who I am."

"What are you trying to say?"

"Take ownership of who you are instead of trying to hide from it." He paused, placed his hands on my cheeks, and kissed me. "You might be surprised at how good you feel about yourself."

CHAPTER TWENTY-ONE

DEVIN

Wearing his Sunday best, Herb surveyed the table. The last time I'd seen him so happy was the day he picked me up from prison. Glowing with a combination of pride and excitement, he put his hands on his hips.

"Damn, this looks good," he said, glancing from one dish to the other. "I can't believe you did this for me."

"You said chicken-fried steak was your favorite, so that's what you're getting."

He looked at Teddi. "I'm not sitting until you do."

She took her seat, glanced at the food, and let out a sigh. "I haven't eaten like this in a long time."

"You look like a few meals wouldn't hurt you any," Herb said. "You're thinner than when I bought this house, that's for damned sure."

"I was going through a phase when you bought this house," she said. "I was on a cookie-and-wine diet."

Herb took his seat. "Don't sound like much of a diet to me."

"I don't know how she stays so small," I said. "You ought to see her eat."

Herb nodded toward the platter of meat. "This stuff's going to get cold if we don't get busy. Get the woman a steak, would ya?"

"I'll get it started." Teddi reached for the serving fork. "Which one do you want, Herb?"

"The big one on your right," he replied. "The one dipshit's eyeing."

Laughing, she lifted the steak from the platter and dropped it onto Herb's plate. "Here you go."

Herb looked at me and grinned. "I saw you eyeballing that thing. Tough luck, asshole."

"Go to hell, old man."

"Lead the way," he said with a laugh.

Teddi's eyes darted back and forth between us. "Are you guys always like this?"

Herb slopped a huge dollop of mashed potatoes on top of his steak. "Like what?"

"Arguing."

Herb chuckled. "This is nothing. When he opines about politics, police, or pussy, we really get going."

Thirty years of cussing in the army was difficult to erase, but we'd discussed being civil during Teddi's debut at Sunday dinner. It was apparent he either didn't care or he'd forgotten our agreement.

"Damn it, Herb," I snapped. "We talked about this. I thought we weren't going to cuss?"

He spooned corn onto his plate like it was his last meal. "Who's cussing?"

"You said *pussy.*"

"Pussy's a body part. It's not a cuss word," he replied without looking up.

"The hell it's not."

He arched a wiry brow. "What else am I going to call it?"

"Hoo-hah," Teddi said.

Herb seemed confused. "Who what?"

"Hah," Teddi said. "A hoo-hah."

Herb looked at me. "Do people call them that?"

I shrugged. "I guess."

"Or a cooch," Teddi said. "You could call it that. Or a muff."

"I've heard that one," Herb said. "On the HBO."

"HBO," I said. "Not *the* HBO. You sound like an imbecile."

He shot me a glare. "Better than looking like a living, breathing dog turd."

"You guys are funny," Teddi said, giving each of us a quick look. "This is fun."

"I don't know that I'd describe anything that included him as being fun," Herb said. "But it's often entertaining."

"How about we agree to cuss," Teddi said, winking at me as she spoke. "We'll just be ourselves."

"Sounds good to me," Herb said. "As long as dipshit agrees to it."

"I'll agree if you can keep it civil," I said.

"Fuck it," Teddi said with a laugh. "It's settled. We're cussing."

Herb poked a piece of gravy-slathered steak into his mouth and looked at Teddi. "You know, when you jumped dipshit's ass in that meeting right after he started, I told him he should have told you to go fuck a goat. Now that I'm getting to know you, hell, I like you."

Teddi smiled. "He was intimidating at first. I overreacted."

"That's not what you said, old man." I gestured to him with the tines of my fork. "But whatever."

"I thought we were being civil?"

"Civil and honest," I said.

Herb swallowed his food and took a drink of tea. He looked at Teddi. "I told him you should fuck a goat." He looked at me. "There, is that better?"

Teddi gasped. "Holy cow."

"Goddammit, old man," I seethed.

He gave me a look. "You said to be honest."

"I meant if you can't be honest, don't speak."

"Well, that's not what you said," he huffed.

"It's fine," Teddi interjected. "I probably would have skull fucked me too."

We all had a laugh and continued with our meals. It was a nice change having Teddi at Sunday dinner. Herb saw us as the children he never had the time to father, and we each saw him as the parent we'd lost at an age earlier than we were prepared to let go.

We talked about *Jeopardy*'s best all-time players, Vanna White's tits, and the recent resurgence of game shows like *Match Game, The $100,000 Pyramid*, and *Let's Make a Deal*. Convinced that there was a place in my life for Teddi and that she was in it, I picked the steak from between my teeth and listened to her and Herb attempt to solve the world's problems.

"I think the government needs to get its hands out of everything," Herb complained. "They overtax us, regulate shit that's none of their business, and can't seem to make decisions when it's high time to do so. Guns, drugs, terrorists, don't get me—"

Herb flinched at the sound of someone pounding on the door.

"Who in the hell could that be?" he asked.

I didn't need to ask. The "cop knock" was all too familiar.

Herb rose from his seat and shuffled to the door. Upon

opening it, he began his tirade.

"What did I tell you the last time you came banging on my door like that?" Herb asked. "What the fuck are you doing here on the Sabbath? Don't you rotten pricks ever take a day off?"

"I need to see Mr. Wallace," my parole officer announced.

Herb leaned to the side, giving a clear view of the dinner table. "There," he said. "You can see him. Now get the hell out of here."

I stood. "It's all right, old man."

"Who is it?" Teddi whispered.

"My parole officer."

"Oh." A worried look washed over her. "Is everything okay?"

"Just a routine call."

"On Sunday?"

"On whatever day they choose, really."

I turned toward the door. "Afternoon, Mr. Jacobs."

He raised a plastic cup. "Can I get a sample?"

"I'll give you a goddamned sample," Herb said. "I'll drop a nice turd in there for you."

"Leave it alone, old man," I said.

"Fuck this asshole," Herb snarled. "I told him the last time he came barging in here to call first."

"That's not how we operate," Jacobs said. "They're surprise visits for a reason."

"Give me your address," Herb said. "I'll pay you a surprise visit while you're enjoying dinner. We'll see how cordial you are." He gave him a once-over. "I bet you're a real fucking treat when you're irritated, huh?"

I nudged Herb away from the doorway. "Come on in."

"Still employed?" he asked.

"Since the report I sent you last week?" I asked with a laugh. "Yes, I am."

"Had any contact with law enforcement?"

"Other than you, no."

"Used any illicit drugs?"

"Sure haven't."

He handed me the cup, which was sealed in a protective plastic bag. "You know the drill."

"Follow me," I said.

He followed me into the bathroom and stood at my side as I gathered the courage to piss in his presence. Federal officers were required to witness the piss leave the tip of your dick and enter the cup without being tampered with.

After I trickled enough urine into the cup for him to test it, I held it at my side. "There you go."

He stretched rubber gloves over his hands and inserted the test strip, waited a moment, and then looked at it. He sealed the strip in a plastic baggie. "You can dump that."

I dumped the cup out in the toilet and then tossed it in the trash.

"You know I don't like this any more than you do," he said.

"No word on my motions?" I asked.

"You'll know at the same time I know," he said. "If not sooner."

"They ask for your recommendation, don't they?"

"I'm not at liberty to say."

It was the standard response from a federal officer when they didn't want to give an answer to a question. I'd spent the last eight and a half years hearing it every time I asked a question, no matter how simple it was.

"I guess I keep applying until they say something one way or another," I said.

"That's my unofficial recommendation." He peeled off his rubber gloves and tossed them in the trash. "What are your plans if they agree to an early release?"

I knew exactly what I was going to do upon my release. I intended to ride across Alligator Alley and return to the club I was forced to abandon. It was none of his business, though.

I zipped my pants and reached for the door. "I'm not at liberty to say."

CHAPTER TWENTY-TWO

TEDDI

Devin stepped into my office. "Everything all right?"

"Absolutely," I said. "Shut the door, if you don't mind."

He closed the door and approached my desk, stopping ten feet from the far side. "What's up?"

I gestured to the chair beside him. "Sit down. Please."

"You sure everything's okay?" he asked. "You look like something's going on in your head."

"Everything is fine," I assured him. "Have a seat."

Balancing my personal life with my professional life wasn't an easy task. As much as I wanted to jump Devin each time he came into my office, I knew better than to get caught up in such antics. There was a time and a place for us to be affectionate toward one another, and it wasn't during work hours or at the office.

"Can you believe it's been three months?" I asked.

He sat down. "What's been three months?"

"Since you came to work here."

"Has it?" He grinned. "Seems like yesterday."

"Are you being serious?"

"I am. It sure doesn't seem like three months have passed." His gaze lowered for an instant, and then he looked at me. "Then again, it sure seems like a lot of stuff has happened since I came to work here. I don't know. Time flies, I guess. Is this my ninety-day review?"

I laughed. "No." I reached for his envelope, flipped it across my desk, and nodded toward it. "That's for you."

He picked it up. "What is it?"

"A bonus, of sorts."

"Bonus?"

"For the Seever residence."

He tossed it at me. "That's ridiculous. I enjoyed it. You don't need to do—"

"I'm not doing anything for you that I wouldn't do for anyone else. There's an equation I use for non-licensed sales, and I've followed it." I tossed the envelope at him. "Open it."

He pulled a knife from his pants pocket. "As long as it's legit."

"It is."

He cut the envelope open, shook out the check, and looked at it. He choked out a cough at his surprise. "Looks like you gave me the wrong check."

"How much is it for?" I asked, trying not to smile.

He lifted it to the light. "Seven hundred and fifty-four grand."

"No," I said. "You got the right one."

His eyes shot wide. "Are you fucking serious?"

"Sorry it took so long," I said. "It's sixty days after everything clears escrow, but it starts on the first of the month following the sale. Anyway. I hope you put it to good use."

He looked at the check and then at me. "This is mine?"

"Every cent of it," I replied. "I want you to know how much I appreciate the hard work."

"I need to give you part of this, for sure."

"Believe me," I said. "I got my part."

He studied the check as if he was unsure that it was real. "Are you sure?"

"The company gets its share, the selling agent gets his, and the listing agent gets hers," I explained. "It's all covered."

"Selling them beats the shit out of building them," he said.

"Get your license," I said. "I could use a construction-savvy agent."

He grinned. "I'm good right where I am for now."

"Well. Congratulations, and thank you, again. I couldn't have done it without you. I wish I could do more, but if I did, it would be unfair."

"More?" He coughed out a laugh. "This is more than I would have expected out of a lifetime of doing what I did. I enjoyed it."

"You still want to go out to eat?" I asked. "Or are you going shopping?"

"Shopping?" He laughed. "I'm not much of a shopper." He glanced at his watch. "I didn't realize it was so late. Let me straighten up my desk and I'll be ready to go."

★ ★ ★

We strolled along the sidewalk at Mercato, one of Naples's open-air shopping areas that included a theater, fine dining, and exquisite shopping. As we walked toward one of my favorite Italian restaurants, Bravo!, we passed Dunkin's Diamonds showroom.

I took a quick glance at a ring that caught my eye in the window. Certain that my interest went unnoticed, I continued my stride at the same pace.

"Do you want to go in?" Devin asked.

"Me?" I asked. "No."

He stopped. "Are you sure?"

"Positive."

"You sure seemed interested in something."

"I just glanced at a—"

"Let's go inside," he said. "You can take a longer look." He nodded toward the restaurant, which was on the other side of the narrow street. "They're not even busy. We've got plenty of time."

I couldn't speak for other women, but for me, looking at diamonds was a love-hate affair. I loved doing it, but afterward, I hated the fact that I didn't have a ring on my finger. I always seemed to slip into a slight state of depression after looking at rings. Each one I saw acted as a reminder that I was perpetually single. Nevertheless, I loved it until I came to that realization.

"Okay," I said. "Just for a minute."

We stepped inside. Necklaces, rings, earrings, and bracelets of every imaginable design, ranging from elegant to gaudy, were on display in the well-lighted cases.

"The ring in the window," Devin said, directing his comment to the middle-aged salesclerk with perfect salt-and-pepper hair. "It looks like an old mine cut. About four carats. Maybe more. Can we see it?"

The suit-wearing salesman smiled at me. "The man knows his diamonds." He looked at Devin. "You've got a keen eye. It is an old mine cut stone. A five-point-two carat center stone, with just over two carats of side stones for a total carat weight of seven-point-two-two carats. The color and clarity are remarkable for an old mine cut."

"What's an old mine cut?" I asked.

"It's the earliest form of brilliant cut, dating back to the early seventeen hundreds," the salesman replied. "The stones were cut in that fashion to allow them to sparkle in even the dimmest of lights."

"I see."

He removed the ring from the display and handed it to me. "This particular piece was obtained through a local family following the downsizing of an estate. We normally don't carry old mine cuts, as they tend to be lesser clarity and often fail to meet our standards in respect to color."

"This is a good one, though?" I asked.

He chuckled and then looked at Devin. "VVS1 clarity with a D color and no fluorescence."

Devin coughed. "Yeah. It's beyond *good*."

I started to slip the ring onto my finger and then paused. "Can I?"

He nodded. "Absolutely."

I slid it onto the ring finger of my right hand. I felt six inches taller, invincible, and, strangely, loved.

An instant of admiration followed, and then I pulled it off like it was on fire. I handed it to the salesclerk.

"It is nice," I said. "Thank you."

He seemed appalled that I didn't enjoy it for longer. "Is there anything else you'd like to see?"

"No," I said, turning away slightly. "We were just on our way to dinner."

He wiped the smudges from the ring with a cloth. "Where are you dining?"

"Bravo!" I said. "Right next door."

"Great choice. I love the calamari."

"Thanks again," I said.

"Absolutely." He reached into his pocket and produced a business card. "I'm James."

"Teddi," I said. "And Devin."

He smiled. "Stop in anytime."

I handed Devin the card and turned toward the door, wishing we hadn't stopped in. The ring was nothing more than a gorgeous reminder that in time, Devin would be with his motorcycle club, I'd be single once again, and I'd never have such a remarkable diamond on my finger unless I bought it myself.

Devin draped his arm over my shoulder as we stepped through the door. "Is everything all right?"

"Fine," I lied. "Just fine."

CHAPTER TWENTY-THREE

DEVIN

Freshly showered and following the lure of frying bacon, I stepped into the kitchen. Wearing a pair of sweats, an old T-shirt, and slippers, Teddi stood in front of the stove, staring into a skillet. Although I wasn't accustomed to the look, it suited her well.

"You look cute," I said.

She glanced at me and smiled. "Thank you."

It seemed something had fallen apart during our dinner date. Short-tempered a little more than normal, less talkative, and lacking interest in sex, she'd gone to sleep without saying much more than *good night* after we returned to her home.

"Did you sleep well?"

"Yeah. You?"

I kissed her neck. "I did."

She wedged my face between her shoulder and her jaw. "Stop it."

"Stop kissing you?"

"Stop kissing my neck," she said. "It drives me nuts."

I pulled away and moved to the other side. I kissed her neck twice, hoping it would bring her out of the foul mood it seemed she'd slipped into.

"I'm going to burn the eggs," she complained.

Her hair was fashioned into some kind of an "I'm in a hurry" bun. Errant strands of blond hair danced at either side of her face as she shuffled from side to side in an effort to escape my attack.

I considered slapping her on the ass but feared doing so wouldn't be well received. Instead, I gave her side-armed hug. "I had a good time last night."

"Yeah," she said. "Me too."

She removed the skillet from the stove and rushed to where she had two plates sitting. She slid eggs onto the plates and handed me one.

"Eat it before it gets cold."

"Perfect timing," I said.

"I started frying the eggs when I heard the shower turn off."

I poured a cup of coffee and joined her at the table. "What's your favorite type of egg?"

"Fried, over medium," she said. "But I rarely eat them that way. Scrambled is the norm around here."

"Why?"

"They're healthier. Less fat."

I gazed across the table at her as I nibbled my bacon. She was a remarkably beautiful woman. I couldn't believe she found interest in me beyond sex. While she fidgeted with her eggs, I realized she wasn't wearing a bra.

It wasn't surprising, considering she was in the privacy of her home. For some reason, however, I was fascinated by it. Her boobs were small by today's "often enhanced" standards but large for her small frame. Swaying from side to side as she cut her toast into bite-sized pieces, they were nothing short of amazing.

My cock began rising against my shorts. Surprised by my unsolicited state of arousal, I began to daydream about playing with Teddi's boobs.

The next thing I knew, my cock was as stiff as a steel rod.

For most men, an erection in such a setting would have been an everyday occurrence. For me, it was a much more noteworthy accomplishment. For as long as I could recall, I needed aggressive sex to obtain an erection. At minimum, the knowledge of rough sex being on the horizon was required.

Yet.

I sat across from Teddi with a stiffy so significant, my head was swimming.

Wondering if the entire thing was nothing but a fluke, I diverted my attention to my food. Mindlessly, I nibbled my toast and ate my eggs, fully expecting the swelling to subside. Ten silent minutes later, my food was gone, and I was still as stiff as a pubescent teen in a strip club.

I glanced at Teddi. She'd eaten her food and was staring blankly at the center of the table. Sporting my embarrassingly rigid hard-on, I stood, grabbed our plates, and took them to the sink. After rinsing them and placing everything in the dishwasher, I was still as erect as if I were face fucking a willing participant who lacked a gag reflex.

I tapped Teddi on the shoulder and tilted my head toward her room. "C'mon."

"C'mon what?" she asked.

I glanced at the horizontal tent I was pitching. Her eyes naturally followed mine.

"What's that about?" she asked.

"That's all you," I said.

She beamed with pride. "Why?"

"Because," I replied. "You're sexy as fuck."

"In this?"

"In anything."

I took her by the hand and led her to the bedroom. In what I expected was part experiment and part wishful thinking, I took a position at her side on the bed. A few minutes of playful kissing followed.

Still as stiff as a stone, I removed my shorts and shirt and tossed them aside. She followed suit, stripping herself of her morning's attire entirely.

I positioned her with her head at the headboard, flat on her back. I nestled myself between her legs and kissed her gently.

In the past, the positioning and the sexual temperature wouldn't have been enough to arouse me more than a soap commercial.

My throbbing cock twitched against her inner thigh, itching to feel the pleasure of her warm confines.

As we kissed, she guided it between her legs. Free of dirty talk, ass slapping, choking, or hair pulling, I carefully slid my length inside.

Not so small that it was uncomfortable but tight enough to evoke caution in my manner of proceeding, her pussy fit me like a custom-made glove.

Nearly overcome with excitement regarding my newfound ability to have meaningful sex, I made love to her like it was my first time. In many respects, it was. My previous sexual encounters, although not in their entirety, had been driven by thoughts of violence, hate, and domination.

The sex that was underway was fueled by nothing other than deep-seated feelings for the woman who lay beneath me.

I made love to her tenderly, and in silence, enjoying the feeling of her naked body against mine. Our two bodies managed to become one, neither of us requiring instruction from the other to proceed with fulfilling our sexual desires.

My forestrokes were met by her aft and vice versa. As if choreographed, we continued, holding one another tightly as our hips moved in perfect timing with one another. I feared if I released her, the magic would somehow come to an end. It was a chance I wasn't willing to take, so I held her like our time together was to be our last.

Each stroke brought me measurably closer to climax. Our eyes met. We didn't speak. Words would have only tarnished an otherwise perfect meeting of two souls meant to share an equally perfect lovemaking session.

As if our lives were connected by a string, we reached climax together as we kissed. When the fireworks ended, I collapsed at her side.

The time to speak was upon me. So I did just that.

"I love you," I said, meeting her content gaze. "I'm sure of it."

"I've been loving you," she said in a shaky voice, "for some time now."

Smiling, I kissed her. My father always said *ladies first*.

CHAPTER TWENTY-FOUR

TEDDI

Herb lifted a forkful of the baked grouper to his mouth. "Best damned fish I've ever eaten, and I've eaten my share, believe me."

Devin claimed that Herb was eighty years old, but one wouldn't think it by looking at him. He would easily be guessed for sixty-five by anyone who met him.

He was physically fit for his age and wasn't overweight or disproportionate in his build. If anything, he still looked as if he were in the military. His aging chest was broad, his waist was trim, and his arms still bore the shape of an athlete regardless of whether or not they were as muscular as they once were.

He always wore khaki-colored polyester pants, a button-down, short-sleeved shirt, and soft-soled walking shoes. In my opinion, he was adorable in looks and in attitude.

I smiled at his remark. "Thank you."

"Can't believe this shit was made in my kitchen."

"It's not where it's made, old man," Devin said. "It's who's making it."

Herb lowered his fork and gave Devin a dirty look. "Would you just shut up for once? Just once? Let me eat in peace."

"If you weren't talking nonsense, we'd all be eating in

silence," Devin retorted. "But you keep saying dumb shit."

"You don't have to correct everything I say," Herb complained.

Having eaten with them on the past four Sundays in a row, I realized their back-and-forth banter was nothing more than playful antics. At first, I didn't know what to think. I now saw it as entertaining and often found myself goading them into an argument if I could.

"Just try to minimize the stupid remarks," Devin said.

Being a part of Herb's weekly routine was something I looked forward to more than I ever would have expected. The death of my parents came at a young age, leaving most of my adult life to be lived without parental figures, family dinners, gift sharing on Christmas, or a celebrated birthday.

Something as simple as Sunday dinner with my biker boyfriend and a retired army veteran was enough to satisfy me to no end.

"Can we make this a tradition?" I asked.

Herb looked up. "This fish? Fuck yes, we can."

I laughed. "I mean the Sunday gatherings."

"I declared it a tradition after the first time you showed up," Herb replied. "I told dipshit if you weren't here on Sundays, he was going to have to find someplace else to live. His tight ass doesn't want to spend a dime if he doesn't have to, so he agreed."

"Is he frugal?" I asked.

Herb barked out a laugh. "Tell her how long you've owned your motorcycle."

I looked at Devin. "How long?"

"Nineteen years."

"Wow. Really?"

He nodded. "Really."

"Ask him about the boots."

His boots were worn, but they couldn't be very old. I asked, nevertheless. "What about the boots?"

"Twelve years," he replied. "Maybe thirteen. They were in a closet for eight of those, though."

"Don't make light of the fact that you're a frugal prick," Herb snarled. "Most men would have tossed those nasty bastards upon receiving an eight-year sentence. What'd he do? He put them in the back closet. He cleans 'em once a week and oils them nearly every night. Man hates to spend money. The thought of it makes him itch."

"Really?" I asked.

Devin nodded. "I've always been this way."

"Have you spent any of your bonus?"

He shook his head. "Not a dime."

"Devin!" My eyes bulged. "You've got to treat yourself."

"To what?" he asked. "I've got everything I need right here."

His reasoning was sweet and difficult to argue with. "I guess saving money is a good thing."

It frustrated me that I'd saved as much as I had and then lost it to a bad investment with an equally bad boyfriend. Although Devin said at one time that he'd take care of it, I realized there was nothing he could do to get the money to reappear.

"You never said what was in the oven," Herb said, glancing over his shoulder. "It's starting to smell good."

"Pie," I said. "Peach. They had fresh ones at a market in Immokalee."

"I was going to have another helping of that rice, but I'm

not going to spoil my appetite," Herb said. "Damned shame we don't have any vanilla ice cream to go with it."

"I brought ice cream," I said. "It's in the freezer."

"You know," he said, giving me a soft look, "when turd bucket told me you swallowed his junk, I told him you were a keeper. Now I'm sure of it."

"Goddammit, Herb," Devin growled. "That's enough."

I coughed on a mouthful of rice until it came out my nose. After making things right again, I looked at Herb with a face that was undoubtedly glowing red. "I can't swallow his junk."

"Spunk," he said. "I get 'em mixed up."

Embarrassed but entertained nonetheless, I laughed out loud. Devin said I needed to own who I was, so I did without hesitation.

"I swallow his spunk because I love him," I said.

His brows pinched together. "He told me all about the declaration of love. From what I understand, you were swallowing that goop long before then." He looked at Devin and then back at me. "Am I wrong?"

"Probably not," I said.

"You swallowed it long before you loved him, right?" he asked.

With anyone else, it would have been awkward. With Herb, it was entertaining. I nodded in agreement to his claim. "I suppose."

"Can I ask you a question about it?" he asked. "An honest one?"

"Sure."

"Does that shit taste good, or does it taste like one would think?"

"I try not to taste it," I said.

"How the hell does one do that? Swallow something without tasting it? Do you plug your nose?"

I laughed. "No. I let it go down my throat. Bypass the tongue, no taste."

He nodded slowly as if he'd finally comprehended the process of splitting an atom. "That makes sense." He looked at Devin. "I told you no one wants to taste that shit."

I looked at each of them and shook my head. "I can't believe you two talk about this kind of stuff."

"I don't think you and Kate are much different," Devin said.

"We're probably not," I admitted.

"Things sure have changed since I was young," Herb said. "Girls didn't talk about spunk, junk, or anything in between. Hell, half of 'em wouldn't put a man's wiener in their mouth if their life depended on it. Now, Vinnie said his granddaughters were doing it in eighth grade." He shook his head. "I think Facebooks and Twitter has everyone messed up in the head."

"You're probably right," I said. "I don't use social media for anything but work, really."

"I find that refreshing," he said. "Gals at the clubhouse sit there all day on their phones, pecking away while they eat lunch. Hell, they don't even talk to each other."

"Sad, isn't it?"

"Damned sure is," he said. "I'll tell you another thing that's changed. Sending those damned messages. Before we were married, when I wanted to talk to Midge, I had to walk to her house. She didn't have a phone, and there were times when we didn't either. Sometimes, I'd walk all the way to her house—three miles, mind you—only to find out she wasn't home. If it was the middle of the night and I thought of something I needed to tell her, I couldn't send her one of those messages. I had to scribble it down on a pad I kept on my nightstand so I didn't forget, and then I'd tell her the next day."

"That's awesome," I said.

"We had three television channels, too. ABC, NBC, and CBS. The big three, that's what we called 'em. That was it, until about fifty years ago, when they added PBS. Now I've got two hundred twenty of 'em, and I can't find a damned thing worth watching. They need to bring *Laugh-In, I Love Lucy, The Carol Burnett Show, The Honeymooners,* and *Archie Bunker* back on TV. Maybe kids would stop shooting up the schools if there was something meaningful to watch."

"I think they'd stop shooting up the schools if their parents paid attention to them."

"You're probably right." He looked at Devin. "See how we do this?"

"Do what?" Devin asked.

"Talk without arguing," Herb replied. "I talk, she talks, I talk, she talks. Neither one of us has to be right, and nobody's wrong. We're just chewing the fat, passing time. You should try it sometime."

"Go to hell, old man."

Herb looked at me. "What about that pie?"

I shot up from my seat. "Oh, crap."

I pulled the pie from the oven just in time. After it cooled a little, I served it warm with two scoops of vanilla ice cream.

Herb ate his slowly, seeming to savor each bite. "Reminds me of Midge's cooking," he said, directing his comment to Devin. "Your cooking reminds me of Tex Miller. That piece of shit couldn't cook to save his respective ass."

"Who's Tex Miller?" I asked.

"Cook in the army," Herb replied. "Lazy bastard had

three dishes he cooked on rotation. Undercooked scrambled eggs, overcooked burgers, and liver and onions. Dipshit here isn't much better. He cooks undercooked burgers, overcooked eggs, spaghetti with store-bought sauce, and a damned fine chicken-fried steak."

"At least he cooks," I said.

He lifted a scoop of pie. "I suppose that's one way to look at it."

Devin glared. "How about you cook next week?"

"How about you pay half the mortgage?" Herb asked.

"How about you kiss my ass?"

"Go fuck a goat," Herb muttered.

I rolled my eyes and stood. "Anyone want seconds?"

Herb raised his spoon. "Right here, sweetheart. When you get to be my age, you learn to appreciate the finer things in life."

"Like what?" I asked.

"Close friends, distant enemies, quiet sunsets, a loud television, a dark room to sleep in, a bright light to read by, something sour with my Scotch, and something sweet with my meal." He looked at each of us and smiled a heartfelt smile. "And the most rewarding thing of all is if that meal is with my family." He handed me his bowl. "Thanks for making this possible, sweetheart."

I took his bowl and quickly turned toward the kitchen. As I filled it with an extra-large piece of pie, a tear escaped my eye.

"I couldn't agree more," I said, wiping it away with the heel of my palm. "Family dinners are hard to beat."

Devin sneaked up behind me and kissed my neck. "Impossible."

CHAPTER TWENTY-FIVE

DEVIN

Taking a piece of advice from the old man, Teddi and I were walking along the beach, barefoot. In a matter of fifteen minutes, the sun would be setting.

"Are you sure no one's going to mess with our shoes?" she asked.

"If there's one thing that won't get messed with, anywhere," I assured her, "it's an old tattered Harley and whatever's hanging from the handlebars."

"You're probably right."

"I know I'm right."

Over the years, I'd parked my motorcycle at bars, restaurants, rural side streets, and busy shopping malls. Not once was it—or whatever was on it or in it—messed with. There was an unwritten code that was understood by bikers and non-bikers alike.

You don't mess with a man's Harley.

We walked along the beach, where the ocean pulsed against the surface of the sand. Every few steps we took, the summer's warm tide cleansed our feet from the grains trapped between our toes. I held Teddi's hand in mine, knowing one thing it would never wash away would be the memories we were making together.

With her designer bags, red-bottom shoes, Range Rover, and the petite gold Rolex watch she often wore, Teddi wasn't at all who I would have expected to fall in love with. I came to believe after meeting Teddi that whom we fall in love with wasn't a conscious choice we made. It merely happened, and it was up to us to recognize it.

Convinced her existence in my life was something I'd somehow earned, I strolled along the beach, wondering just what that something might have been.

Although I'd never been what I would describe as a bad person, I wasn't a good one by anyone's definition either. My trip to prison might have been unwarranted for the crime I'd been charged with, but there were several other crimes I'd escaped conviction on during my tenure as an outlaw biker.

Teddi tugged against my hand. "Look," she said, facing the horizon. "It's happening."

The sun fell behind a ribbon of low-lying clouds. The sky behind her illuminated. Orange and purple hues replaced the evening's powder-blue landscape. Pink melded in, casting a reflection on the ocean's surface worthy of praise.

"It's beautiful," she said.

I studied the silhouette of her face. The breathtaking colors that spread along the horizon went out of focus. The image I was left with was nothing short of awe-inspiring.

"It sure is," I said in agreement, although we were talking about two different things.

We gazed at the horizon until the sky darkened to indigo. Speechless, we faced each other and kissed.

"I love you," she said.

I swept her hair behind her ear with the tip of my finger. "I love you too."

"I want to thank you again for allowing me into Herb's life. I adore that guy."

"Thanks for putting up with him."

"He's easy."

I took her hand in mine and walked up the beach, toward where we'd parked the motorcycle. Mixed in with the vacationers, lovestruck teens, and others just like us, we worked our way to the boulevard that followed the shore.

"My life is nothing short of perfect," she said.

"Do you believe that?" I asked.

"I do."

"You need nothing?"

"Need?" she asked. "No."

"Want?" I asked.

"A girl always wants," she replied.

"What? What does a girl always want?"

"A sense of security," she said. "Reassurance that what she has won't fade away. To be reminded from time to time that she's loved. Things like that."

"Do I provide those things?"

She smiled. "You do."

"So, what is it that you want?"

"Now? Nothing."

"If that changes, will you let me know?"

She grinned. "I'll keep you posted."

We reached the parking lot where the motorcycle was parked. On both sides of it, other motorcycles had been parked, each making use of the minimal space that was available along the beach at sunset.

"They kind of boxed you in," she said.

Seeing them reminded me of the many times we'd done

similar things while out on the road and unable to find a spot to park. I missed the men in the club. The comradery. The brotherhood. The sense of belonging.

"Do you miss them?" she asked.

I realized I was staring blankly at the row of motorcycles.

"Who?" I asked, although I knew what she was asking.

"The guys in your MC?"

I nodded. "I do."

"The guy who came to Herb's house won't let you go see them?" she asked. "Your parole officer?"

"No," I replied. "He won't."

"That's dumb."

"Yeah, it is."

She took her sneakers off the handlebars and untied the laces. "It won't last forever."

"One of these days, I'll be able to go where I want, when I want, with who I want."

She leaned against the motorcycle and slipped on her shoes. "When you're given that freedom, what will change?"

I couldn't give an answer because I didn't know. I'd spent eight years with the belief that nothing was more important than returning to the club. I now wondered if my priorities were in line with what my life's necessities truly were.

"I don't know," I replied.

For the time being, what was in front of me was all that was important or necessary. I hoped that no amount of freedom would change that, but I had no way of knowing. So I clung to the belief that what satisfied me at that moment would continue to satisfy me forever.

CHAPTER TWENTY-SIX

TEDDI

Kate pinched a piece of sushi between her chopsticks and lifted it to her mouth. "The craziest?"

"Absolute craziest."

"Crazy how?"

I sipped my sake. "Something that surprised the hell out of you. In a good way."

She wedged the slice of sushi into her mouth. As she chewed, she rocked her head from side to side goofily.

"I suppose," she said, still chewing the food, "it'd have to be anal beads."

I nearly choked. I leaned over the edge of the table. "Anal beads?" I whispered excitedly. "Oh my God. When?"

"I don't know. It doesn't matter."

"It does," I argued. "Who was it with?"

She reached for her drink. "It doesn't matter."

I relaxed against the back of my chair and gave her a side-eyed look. "We're keeping secrets now?"

"Fine. It was a few weeks ago."

I gasped. "You're seeing someone?"

She picked up another piece of sushi. "Kind of."

I slapped her hand. "Stop eating. Tell me more."

"I met him at Cavo."

"You went there without me?"

Her brows pinched together. "You're going clubbing with me now? You and Devin?"

I let out a sigh. "Good point. Anyway..." I finished my sake. "Give it to me."

I raised my glass. She lifted the flask and poured me another. "He's older than me, and he—"

"How much older?"

"Ten years."

"Okay, go ahead."

"He's thinking about moving here. He was—"

"He doesn't live here?"

"No."

"You had a one-night stand that included anal beads?" I gave her a look. "Who are you?"

"I've seen him ten times, give or take. The first time was three weeks ago."

"What's he do?"

She chuckled. "It's kind of funny."

"Funny how?"

"Well." She sipped her sake until it was gone. "He's a drug dealer. Kind of."

"A pharmaceutical rep?"

"No." She raised her glass. "A drug dealer."

I eagerly poured it until it overflowed. "A pharmacist?"

She shook her head. "Drug. Dealer."

"A fucking drug dealer?" I whispered. "Like, drugs?"

"Kind of."

"What does that mean?"

"He sells CBD oil."

Disappointment washed over me. I scoffed. "CBD is legal. Everywhere. All fifty states."

"But it's still drugs."

I picked up a piece of sashimi with my fingers. "So is Tylenol."

"Well, he's originally from San Diego, and he's kind of a hippy. He's got long hair, he doesn't always shave, and he—"

"Does he stink?"

"What?"

I bit the sashimi in half. "Stink. Does he smell like poop?"

She laughed. "No. He's—"

"Does he wear clean clothes?"

"He's a businessman," she said, clearly defending him. "He dresses nicely. In his own way but nicely."

"Does he have a big dick?"

She coughed out of surprise and leaned forward. "It's as thick as my wrist," she whispered. "I compared them one night."

"Devin's is the size of a fucking cucumber." I poked the other half of the sashimi in my mouth. "One of the big ones. Every time he fucks me, it's like the first time all over again."

"Oh my God," she said. "That's exactly how it is with Forrest."

I laughed. "His name is Forrest?"

"Stop it. I like it. Forrest Cambridge."

I nearly choked on my sashimi. "That's like an oxymoron. First name hillbilly, last name wealth."

She crossed her arms. "I like it."

I grabbed another piece of sashimi. "Tell me about the beads."

"We met at the bar and immediately hit it off. His hair is kind of long, almost to his shoulders. It's all one length, and he wears it back—"

"Beads," I said, rolling my hand in a circular motion. "We can come back to all this."

She shot me a glare. "Thanks for caring."

"This always happens with you," I complained. "We start talking about something, and the next thing I know, we're discussing San Diego's skyline, and I can't remember what it was that we were originally talking about. I end up mad at myself because I can't remember, and I can't remember because you go off on some tangent about something completely unrelated to the subject I wanted to talk about. We were talking about crazy sex. Beads, bitch," I said with a laugh. "Let's hear it."

"It was on the second night we were together. He—"

"Second time you two met, or was it two consecutive nights?"

"Why?" she asked.

"Because. I want to know."

"Two consecutive nights."

I smiled. "Awesome. Go ahead."

"He asked me if I was interested in experimenting. He'd explained on the night we met that he was open-minded. So, on night two, he asked if I was open to experimenting."

"Did you two bone on the first night?"

"We did."

"Basically, you're a whore," I said dryly. "You know that, right?"

"Shut up. You used to screw guys and give them Theresa Bianchi's business card. Don't talk to me about being a whore."

I poked the remainder of sashimi in my mouth and smiled. "Ouch."

"On the second night, I agreed to try the anal beads. I

figured what the hell. You and Devin are fucking in your office, and he's choking you until you nearly pass out. You screwed in the grocery store parking lot, for Christ's sake."

"And?"

"I have to hear all those stories," she said. "I wondered what I might be missing."

"Back to the beads. Did he have them in his suitcase? He probably doesn't have a suitcase, does he? Backpack. Did he have them in his backpack?"

"We bought them in Fort Myers."

"We? You went to a sex shop?"

She grinned. "I did."

"That's disgusting. Were there dildos everywhere?"

"Everywhere. Purple. Black. Pink. Big. Small. Curved. Even ones with little curvy things attached to them." She glanced over each shoulder and then leaned forward. "Two holes at once."

I rolled my eyes. "I'm aware."

"They even have them set up by the cashier, like the candy bars at the grocery store. In case you forget you needed one while you were shopping."

"So you bought the beads. Then what?"

"We were doing it doggy style, and just as I reached climax, he tugged on the little string. They came popping out of there like *pop! pop! pop!* I came so hard, I nearly passed out."

"Holy shit," I blurted. "I just thought of something."

"What?"

"Devin poked his finger up my ass. Just as I was coming. Like, right at that instant. I thought I was going to freaking die. I came so hard, I went blind for a minute. And deaf. I'm so not kidding. My ears went blank. I couldn't hear a damned thing, and we were in the loudest movie in the history of movies."

"You had sex at the theater?"

"A few weeks ago. I forgot to tell you."

She scrunched her nose. "He poked his finger in your butt?"

I nodded. "Just as I started to have an orgasm."

"In the theater?"

"It was my sex-on-command request."

"I thought you were going to do sex on the beach?"

"The sand-in-the-twat thing freaked me out. That stuff gets in everything, no matter how many blankets you take. You know how it is."

"Yeah."

"Anyway. Yeah. The finger-in-the-butt-trick was awesome."

"Oddly," she said, "I just read an article about that."

"About what?"

"Inserting a finger into the anus at climax."

"In what?" I asked with a laugh. "*Penthouse Forum*?"

"*Cosmo.*"

"Oh." I chuckled. "Maybe he reads *Cosmo.*"

She shrugged. "Maybe."

"So, what about this hippy?" I asked. "What's the latest?"

"He's looking at houses next week."

"Where?"

"Old Naples."

"Oh, wow. The CBD business must be good."

"Real estate is considerably less expensive here than it is in San Diego," she said. "His home in La Jolla sold for seven million."

"He already sold it?"

"On Monday."

"I hope everything works out."

She smiled. "Me too. You'll like him. He's pretty laid-back."

"But he doesn't stink?"

She slapped the back of my hand. "Don't be mean."

I reached for my sake. "You know what?"

"What?"

"I'm not as bitchy now that Devin and I are together. I used to constantly be running around, mad at the world, and now I couldn't care less. I'm happy all the time, no matter what happens at work."

"That's awesome."

"I love him," I said.

"I know," she said with a smile. "I can see it. In both of you."

I reached for her hand. "Thank you."

She gave me a confused look. "For what?"

"Doing everything you did," I replied. "You set this up. Don't act like you didn't."

"I wanted you to be happy. You've been so sad for so long. I couldn't stand to see it any longer."

"Well, thank you."

She squeezed my hand. "You're welcome."

CHAPTER TWENTY-SEVEN

DEVIN

Half-soaked from the evening's sporadic rainstorms, I set my keys on the credenza and peered into the living room. "Be right back. I need to change."

Herb looked up.

His face was long and sorrowful.

I paused. "What's wrong, old man?"

"Change your clothes before you drip on my floor."

"What the fuck's wrong with you?"

"Not a goddamned thing wrong with me, dipshit," he snapped back. "Change your clothes."

The afternoon card game must have been canceled. Maybe Vinnie was sick. Something had the old man aggravated, that much was obvious. Instead of poking the bear, I sauntered to my room, changed clothes, and meandered into the kitchen.

"What do you want for dinner?" I asked.

"Already ate," he muttered.

I walked to the edge of the living room and gave him a shitty look. "What do you mean?"

"I stuffed food into my mouth with a fork."

I noticed he was staring at the television and that it was off. "Why?"

"Because I was hungry."

"Is the TV broken?"

"Not that I know of."

"Why are you staring at it?" I asked. "It's off."

He reached for the remote and switched it on. "There. Happy now?"

"I'd be happier if you told me what was going on."

"Nothing's going on," he replied. "I'm just sitting here."

"Doing what?"

"Thinking."

"About what?"

"Life."

I walked to the chair across from him and sat down. "Talk to me, old man. What's going on?"

He reached to his side. With an envelope clutched in his hand, he stood and walked to where I sat. His eyes were welled with tears.

He tossed the envelope into my lap. "Here you go."

I looked at the envelope. The return address was the United States District Court for the Middle District of Florida. Excitedly, I flipped it over. Scotch tape secured the envelope's flap.

"You opened it already?" I asked.

"Just read the damned thing."

Nervously, I removed the letter and unfolded it.

Mr. Wallace,

Regarding your request for early termination from supervised release, we offer the following response.

The court is required to act in accordance with the procedures and allowances set forth in 18 U.S.C. § 3583(e). Pursuant to the aforementioned section, we have carefully considered your request. The below ruling will be entered and in effect on the date of this letter's writing.

You are hereby released from your requirement to report to an officer of the court.

Respectfully,

Jonas Webster, Circuit Judge, Middle District of Florida

"I'm free." I looked at Herb. "Holy. Shit."

"Yeah. Holy shit is right." He looked at me with sad eyes. "What now?"

My mind was going a hundred miles an hour. "I don't know," I stammered.

"You going to Miami to be with those fuck bubbles you used to run with?"

I had no idea what I was going to do. Being free of the court's restrictions, I felt I needed to run in a dozen different directions.

I hated seeing Herb in the condition he was in, but there was nothing I could do or say that would satisfy him. I needed to think, and there was only one way for me to clear my mind to do so.

"You've eaten?" I asked.

"I have."

"I'm going for a ride."

"To Miami?"

"Not sure, old man. I'll see where the road takes me."

"I've got one thing to say before you go," he said.

"What's that?"

"One person got you to this juncture in your life. You need to remember to dance with the one who brought you, son." He turned away. "That's the only advice I've got."

★ ★ ★

At eighty miles an hour, each raindrop felt like a dagger piercing my skin. The torrential downpour had been going on for thirty minutes. Gripping the handlebars like my life depended on it, I held the motorcycle between the white lines, praying the rain would stop before a passing motorist inadvertently forced me into the swamps of the Everglades.

To pass the time—and to take my mind from the pain of riding through a tropical storm—I thought of my future with Teddi's firm. In a million years, I would have never chosen a career in real estate.

I couldn't decide if I enjoyed it because it was all I had or if it was because it was where I belonged.

I considered the MC and the brotherhood the club offered me. Having no family was a difficult pill to swallow. The club resolved the issue as completely as possible. There was no loneliness in an MC, that was for sure.

As much as I enjoyed Herb's company, allowing myself to get closer to him would only hurt me in the future. He wasn't going to live forever. If I stayed where I was for much longer, losing him would crush me.

The rain stopped. Drenched to the bone, I held the handlebars with one hand while removing my glasses with the other.

I wiped them against my jacket, which only made matters worse. An illuminated sign on the horizon marked the distance to my destination.

As I sped past it, I grinned.

MIAMI 12

CHAPTER TWENTY-EIGHT

TEDDI

Harry Morgan sat across from me with his legs crossed. His neatly trimmed gray hair was held into place with product, giving it a sculpted look of sophistication that went well with his custom-tailored suit.

"Let's list it for what I paid for it," he said. "It should sell promptly at that price."

"With all due respect," I said, "I think you could get five million on top of that, if not more. You bought it right after the market collapsed. It's recovered considerably since then."

"I'll go with your recommendation," he said with a nod. "Now, what about a new home? We'd like something close to the beach but not beachfront. Maybe right off Pine Ridge, along Crayton Road."

"Devin's father built several homes along Crayton, believe it or not."

"That's what he said," Harry replied. "He sent me a few listings in that area last week. There's one I'd like to see, for sure. Where is Devin today?"

"He's sick," I said. "It must be pretty bad. He hasn't missed a day since he started. Always the first one in and the last to leave."

"He's a fine example of the old adage, 'You can't judge a

book by its cover.' I knew after a few seconds of talking to him that he was a damned good man. Character can't be disguised as being anything but what it is. His tattoos are a facade."

"He's one of a kind," I agreed. "That's for sure."

"Are you aware of the listings he sent me?" he asked.

I wasn't aware that Devin was communicating with Harry. It didn't surprise me, though. Devin wasn't one to brag or make small talk about upcoming events, listings, or potential clients. He simply did his job and allowed his work to speak for itself.

"Not fully," I replied. "Why do you ask?"

"Of the listings Devin sent, there is one on Crayton and one on Turtle Hatch that appeal to us. Both of them appear to suit our needs. Pricing is commensurate with their location and recent listings in the area, according to the spreadsheet he prepared. I'd like to set up a time to see them."

"Can you forward the addresses to me?"

"I will."

"I'll make the inquiries. We should be able to before the end of the day. Tomorrow at the latest."

"Any word on when Devin will be back?" he asked. "I'd like his opinion on the standard of construction used for each of them."

"I'm sure he'll be back tomorrow."

"Let's make sure he's scheduled to go with us," he said. "I've waited this long. Another day or two won't hurt me."

"I'll make contact with the owners and with Devin, and I'll be in touch. How's that?"

He stood. "Perfect." He gave a nod. "As always, Teddi, it was a pleasure."

"Likewise," I said.

I escorted him to the door and wished him well. As his Rolls Royce pulled away, I peered into the parking spot that Devin had taken ownership of upon arrival. It seemed strange to see it vacant.

I went to my office, got my phone, and sent him a text.

> *Hope everything's okay. Let me know if*
> *you need anything. :)*

I placed the phone on the corner of my desk and began my queries into the homes Harry referenced. I then began searching for similar homes in the area. Phone calls to prospective sellers followed, hoping they'd reached a point that they were ready to sell. In what seemed like no time, the day had escaped me.

Janine stepped into my office and cleared her throat. "Where's your boyfriend?"

"Devin?" I asked.

She cocked her hip and gave me a look. "He's your boyfriend, isn't he?"

"He is."

"Where the fuck is he?"

"Sick. Why?"

"He was doing something for me. I wanted to know if it was done."

"What was it?"

"What's it matter?" she asked, her voice taking on a tone of irritation.

Her New Jersey attitude was often more than I could stomach, but she was a great worker. The East Coast clients loved her. I was surprised that Devin could work with her;

then again, he seemed to get along with all walks of life.

"I guess it doesn't," I said. "I was just wondering."

"He's good with compiling data," she said. "He's making me a spreadsheet of homes and the clients' names for certain dates and price ranges so I could call them to see if they were ready to upgrade." Her brows raised. "Satisfied?"

I laughed. "Sure."

"When's he coming back?"

"Tomorrow, I suppose."

"He better," she said. "I need that spreadsheet."

She stomped off in a huff. I reached for my phone and checked my text messages, only to find that Devin hadn't responded.

If he was too sick to respond, he was too sick to visit. The best thing for him was to allow him to get his rest. I hadn't spent a night alone in months and wondered what I should do with my time.

I lifted the receiver of my desk phone and buzzed Kate's office.

"Kate Winslow," she said.

"This is Teddi, dork."

"Oh, hey. What's up?"

"Want to go out after work?"

"I can't. Forrest is in town."

"Crap."

"Sucks, doesn't it?" she asked.

"What?"

"When they're gone."

"Yeah," I said, releasing a sigh. "It sure does."

CHAPTER TWENTY-NINE

DEVIN

"Where the fuck you been?" Herb asked, nodding toward my backpack. "And where the fuck are you going?"

I'd hoped I could get out of the house before he got home from playing cards but didn't have such luck. "It's best you don't know."

"You're living under my roof," he snarled. "I have a right to know."

"It's best you don't, old man. Believe me."

He gestured toward the backpack. "What's in the rucksack?"

"I'd rather not say."

He gave me a cross look. "You back to your old bullshit?"

"I've got some business to take care of."

"At nighttime? You're back to busting skulls for that ragtag bunch of fuck nuggets in Miami, aren't you?"

"Like I said, I've got some business to take care of. It's best that you know nothing about it."

"Since when do we keep secrets from each other?" he asked.

"Since telling you what I'm doing would make you aware of the commission of a crime."

★ ★ ★

There were a dozen different ways to resolve the issue I was faced with. None of them were wrong. They were all potentially effective, but one stood out as having a far greater rate of success. As with most criminal operations, it had risks associated with it that the other options didn't.

The risk wasn't my concern. Success was.

Thirty minutes of surveillance informed me that he was home alone. My previous visit to the unattended home confirmed there was no alarm system, *Nest* doorbell, or security systems in place.

Based on that belief, I planted the heel of my boot against the back door, just beside the knob. The doorframe splintered into shreds, and the door flew open, hitting the adjoining wall with a *thwack!*

I took long strides through the kitchen and into the living room.

He jumped up from the couch with eyes as wide as saucers. "What—"

I struck him on the cheek with the butt of the pistol. He fell to the floor between the coffee table and the couch.

"Who the hell—"

I grabbed a fistful of his hair and lifted him to his feet. "I talk, you listen. Understood?"

He nodded. "Yes."

I hit him again, splitting a gash open on his cheek. "I talk. You listen. If I want you to speak, I'll let you know."

Wincing in pain, he wiped the blood from his cheek.

"Are you alone?"

I'd seen no one else in my surveillance, but I needed to know for sure.

He nodded.

"You have something I need," I explained. "If you provide it, I will leave, and you'll likely never see me again. If you do not provide it, I will kill you. This is not negotiable. Provide it or die. Those are the only options. Understood?"

He nodded frantically.

"Through the course of our discussions, if you lie to me about anything, I will shoot you in your left thigh. This is also nonnegotiable. Lie to me, get shot. Understood?"

He blubbered as he nodded his response.

"Lastly, if this matter is resolved to my liking but you decide at any time to go to the police, you will be killed. Don't think that if I'm arrested, this step will not be taken or that you can save yourself from this fate. There are thirty-two men just like me who will line up to wipe your existence from this earth. Understood?"

He began to cry.

"I need you to acknowledge what I've said," I warned. "Talk to the cops, you die. Understood?"

He nodded.

"Where's your phone?" I asked. "You may speak."

"It's . . . the end table," he stammered. "Over there."

"Do you have a surveillance system? You may speak."

"No."

"Any cameras?"

He shook his head.

I released his hair and pointed the silenced Walther .22 pistol at his thigh. "You took approximately seven hundred thousand dollars from Teddi Mack. I need that money returned, no exceptions. If you return it, I will leave. If you do not, you will die."

He swallowed heavily. "I don't have it with me."

"I'll wait until you do."

"I can't. There's no way I can get it right now."

I gestured to the couch with the pistol's barrel. "Have a seat."

He flopped onto the couch. I took his phone from the end table and put it in my front pocket. After taking a seat across from him, I warned him of what the future held.

"I'm not going to give you a month, a week, or even a day to get the money. If I don't have it by noon tomorrow, you'll be in the *Naples Daily News* headlines as being murdered by a burglar. You may speak if you think it'll help you explain this matter."

He drew a deep breath and then let it out slowly. "I can get the money, but it won't be easy."

"I don't give a fuck how you get it," I said. "But you need to have it by noon, tomorrow. That, Britt, is not negotiable."

He sighed. "I can have it by noon."

He was lying, and I was sure of it. There was a way to extract the truth. It was time for me to play that card.

"Let's hope for your mother's sake that you're right." I coughed a dry laugh and gave him a sinister look. "Oh, shit. I left that part out, didn't I?"

His eyes widened with wonder.

I reached into my left pocket, removed a small sheet of folded paper, and unfolded it. "Katherine Denton, 11725 Peachtree, Tampa, Florida." I looked up. "Wasn't easy finding her, as your last names don't coincide with one another. She fits into this scenario as well. I've got someone sitting outside her place now. I can't believe I left that out. You've probably never done anything like this, but it's not as easy as you'd think. There's always something you forget. It's got to be the overabundance of adrenaline."

"Before you shoot me," he blurted, "I didn't lie."

"About?"

"The money's upstairs," he said. "I didn't tell you it wasn't here. I said I didn't have it. I don't. It's upstairs."

I waved the pistol's barrel toward the staircase.

Ten minutes later, I had seven hundred and forty thousand dollars in my backpack, and Britt was seated at his desk typing a letter of apology.

"I don't need details," I said. "I need it to be brief, to the point, and for you to fully admit what you did was planned and not a mistake."

He typed the letter, printed it, and handed it to me.

Teddi,

I can't apologize enough for what I have done to you. My decision to swindle you out of your money was done out of greed and nothing else.

The passing of time has forced me to dwell on the decision I made and on the damage that it has likely done to your psyche to have lost so much without knowledge of the truth.

Guilt now forces me to return your initial investment. Please consider my apology as being heartfelt.

My sincere apologies,

Britt

"Add a sentence that says, 'Considering all things, please make no effort to contact me regarding this matter or for any other reason. I will extend the same consideration to you,' or something like that."

Upon reading the amended letter, I folded it neatly. "My work's done here. Don't forget what I told you. Talk to the cops, or anyone for that matter, and your mother—and you—will be killed."

"Understood."

"Like the letter says, make no efforts to contact Teddi again," I said. "Period. If you have a deal that involves her, send one of your underlings. If you walk through the threshold of her office door again, you'll find the barrel of this pistol in your mouth."

"I'll avoid her," he said. "Believe me."

I'd been in similar situations several times in my life. I had a knack for knowing when someone was telling the truth and when someone was lying. He was telling the truth.

"I strongly suggest you find another way to supplement your income," I said. "If you keep this up, you never know who you might piss off."

★ ★ ★

I placed the box on Teddi's porch and rang the doorbell. After ten minutes, I rang it again. Five minutes later, I rang it repeatedly.

From behind her neighbor's shrubs, I waited with bated breath.

The porch light illuminated. The door opened. Her eyes shot to the box. She then searched the dark neighborhood with her eyes, looking for who might have left it. After seeing no one, she opened the box and peered inside.

She removed the letter and read it. She lifted the

newspaper that covered the money. Following another quick scan of the neighborhood, she went inside and shut the door.

I felt terrible for postponing the resolution of the issue. As important as it was to Teddi, I couldn't force myself to proceed any sooner than I had. I knew myself well enough to know the negotiation could have easily turned violent. Taking that risk wasn't something I was willing to do.

I now looked at matters completely differently. Not because of my newfound freedom.

Because things had changed.

CHAPTER THIRTY

TEDDI

I turned the corner onto Herb's street. Upon seeing his home, I gasped. Kate's Lexus, Rhea's SUV, Evelyn's Saturn, Janine's Jag, and Vinnie's Cadillac were all parked in front of the house.

I hadn't seen Devin in three days. We were supposed to have Sunday dinner with Herb and retire early, as Devin's stomach was still bothering him. My heart palpitated as I crept closer to the home. The only reason I could think of why Devin would want such a gathering was to announce having been released from the federal government's custody.

If that were the case, I feared he'd soon be leaving. For good.

We had yet to discuss his intentions at length. It was easy, however, to see where his heart was. When he so much as saw other motorcycles, his eyes lit up with a passion like no other.

With reluctance, I parked my SUV. Following a silent prayer, I got out and walked to the door. It opened before I knocked.

Herb answered. He opened his arms wide, offering a hug. He looked like he'd been crying. My bottom lip quivered in anticipation of what was undoubtedly headed my direction.

I hugged him, holding the embrace for longer than I probably should have. I'd become accustomed to our Sunday dinners together and viewed us as a family. I wondered if Herb would consider allowing me to come after Devin's departure. I decided asking would be out of place.

He looked me in the eyes when I broke the embrace.

"Have you been crying?" I asked. "You look like—"

He wiped his eyes. "Is it obvious?"

"Oh my God," I breathed in an uneven voice. "Herb . . . is . . . Is everything okay?"

"I can't speak for anyone other than my damned self," he said. "I think I'll be just goddamned fine. Come in, sweetheart."

I stepped inside and scanned the living room. Standing between Kate and Vinnie was a handsome man with a deep tan and shoulder-length hair. I nearly started blubbering at the thought of Kate being in a relationship and me loving a man who lived on the other side of the state.

I stumbled throughout the house looking for Devin, only to find that he wasn't in attendance. According to Herb, he was taking care of some last-minute affairs before dinner.

Rhea stood over the stove with Evelyn at her side. The smell of her native cuisine hung in the air like a heavenly fog. I meandered to her side.

"Do you know what's going on?" I asked.

"I was told Devin has an announcement he's going to make," she said. "That's all I know. Herb said he wanted everyone he's been working with to be here for dinner. I volunteered to cook at the last minute."

"Where's Devin?" I asked.

She stirred a boiling pot. "I think he's in Miami."

My heart sank into the pit of my stomach. "Miami?" I asked, nearly bringing myself to tears. "Are you sure?"

"Pretty sure," she replied. "I heard Vinnie talking to

Kate's boyfriend. Why?"

"I was just..." I swallowed against the bile that rose into my throat. "Wondering."

The thought of living without Devin was crippling. Just a day earlier, Britt had returned my money, along with a letter of apology admitting what he'd done wrong. I wanted to tell Devin in person but now wondered if it would even be possible.

Be it the spices in the air, the fact that Devin was with his MC, or that I didn't have a single picture of us together, I'd never know. But I began to softly cry and had to excuse myself to the bathroom.

I stared in the mirror and wondered how I'd allowed myself to make such a mistake. No matter how many times I went over it in my head, I couldn't force myself to believe anything I'd done should have been done differently. I had no regrets.

Only heartache.

After wiping my tears and fixing my makeup, I checked myself in the mirror. I looked like a blond raccoon. Frustrated that I'd be incapable of masquerading my sadness, I dabbed concealer under my eyes.

The wall-mounted mirror began to shake. The faucet followed. A horrendous thunder began to shake the floor beneath my feet.

The sky was clear when I showed up. It was only fitting that a hurricane would crop up out of nowhere and ruin the evening for everyone else.

I burst from the bathroom, certain the end was imminent.

The thunderous noise grew louder with each passing second. By the time I'd reached the living room, the entire group was gathered at the window, peering outside.

"What's going on?" I asked, still standing in the hallway, petrified. "What's happening?"

Vinnie stepped to the side, giving me a view of what they were gawking at. I wouldn't have guessed it could get worse, but it did.

Instantly.

Motorcycles lined both sides of the street. Tattooed men in black vests dismounted their Harleys and hugged one another, slapped each other's backs, and extinguished their cigarettes.

I watched with balled fists as dozens upon dozens of men filtered toward the door. In the middle of the crowd, one stood out above all the rest. I almost didn't recognize him, as he was wearing his motorcycle gang's leather vest.

Devin.

It was apparent his decision was made. Anger built within me until I shook.

The door opened. One by one, leather-clad bikers entered the home. The smell of cowhide, gasoline, and adrenaline wafted past me.

As soon as Devin cleared the doorway, I pushed my way through the crowd. When our eyes met, he looked away. If I learned nothing else from Devin, I learned to be myself. Biting my tongue wasn't an option.

"Really?" I spat. "Really?"

Standing nervously beside two of his MC brethren, he pushed his hands into his pockets. Seeing the patches on the front of his vest—BONE and SERGEANT AT ARMS—made me want to vomit. The battle for his heart had been won, and it was clear I wasn't the victor.

"Teddi, wait," he said. "I can explain."

"If you've got something to say, say it," I snapped back.

"I'm not interested in doing this."

He pushed his way through the crowd. "Doing what?"

"These people. All these people." My eyes welled with tears. "Is this necessary?"

He stepped in front of me. "I needed the men—"

"Fuck them," I blurted. "What about me? I love you, Devin."

Confusion washed over him. "I love you, too."

"Then why?" I asked.

"Teddi—"

"Why?" I demanded, sputtering like a child. "Why all the people? Just to tell me you're leaving?"

"Will you let me talk?"

I shot him a glare. "Talk."

"I had an announcement to make," he said nervously. "Like it or not, these men are my family. I wanted them to be here to—"

"Make it," I demanded.

He gave me a look. "Excuse me?"

"Just say it," I said, cocking my hip. "Have the guts to say it."

"Right now?"

I crossed my arms over my chest and gave a nod. "Right fucking now," I said, not bothering to wipe away the tear that trickled down my cheek.

"Tank!" he bellowed, turning his head to the side. "Front and center!"

Frank shoved his way through the crowd. Devin turned around and whispered something. Frank extended his clenched fist. Devin pounded his knuckles against Frank's before facing me.

"I'm sorry for the confusion," Devin said. "I haven't been sick for the past few days. I've been busy getting things in order. A lot has happened. I've decided to make some changes."

It was painfully obvious he was making changes. I needed to know exactly what they were. It was the only way I could come close to forgiving myself for falling head-over-heels for a man who was married to a motorcycle gang.

"What are they?" I asked.

"I'm turning in my kutte," he said.

"I don't know what that means."

"I'm quitting the club," he explained. "No more MC."

The truth was miles from reality. My lips parted slightly. I wanted to apologize for my preconceived notions but couldn't get my thick tongue to cooperate.

"I'm getting my Realtor's license," he continued. He reached behind his back. Smiling, Frank the Tank handed him something. Devin clasped his open palm over his clenched fist. "I'd like for you to answer a question."

I mouthed the word *okay*.

"A life without you in it isn't one I want to live." He opened his hand. The ring from Dunkin's Diamonds glistened in his flattened palm. "Will you end a lifetime of misery and agree to marry me?"

My knees buckled. While thirty onlookers waited for my response, I stumbled toward the bathroom like a drunken sailor.

Herb caught me before I tumbled to the floor. He held me upright. "Damn it, woman," he said. "Say *something*."

I'd waited a lifetime for the moment to arrive, and it was now before me. I swallowed a ball of nervous apprehension and met Devin's curious gaze.

"Yes," I said. "I will."

Devin slipped the ring onto my finger. A nervous sigh escaped him. "I was beginning to wonder."

"You're not the only one," Herb chimed.

Devin and I embraced in a kiss. When our lips parted, my tear-filled eyes scanned the crowd. Smiles, tears, laughter, and raised fists—many of which were covered with tattoos— filled the living room.

It was an eclectic group to say the least, but they were now my family.

A family I was proud to call my own.

ALSO AVAILABLE FROM
WATERHOUSE PRESS

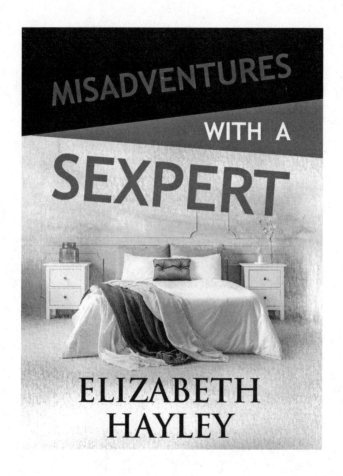

Keep reading for an excerpt!

EXCERPT FROM
MISADVENTURES WITH A SEXPERT

"Isla? It's so nice to meet you. I'm sorry I'm late." After letting go of my hand, he pointed to the empty chair across from me. "May I sit?"

"Yes. Of course. Please."

We looked at each other for a few moments before he spoke. "Sorry if I'm staring," he said. "It's just that you're even more beautiful in person than you are in your pictures."

That made me smile, and I felt the comment draw some heat to my cheeks, no doubt bringing color to my usually pale skin.

"Thank you. I was thinking the same." It was probably the first time any of the men looked better in person than they did in their profile pictures. His short blond hair was a bit longer now, revealing some cute curls in the back, and he definitely didn't skip chest day at the gym.

He looked at me a little longer before I asked if he wanted to get something to drink before we talked.

He nodded. "Sure, I'll grab something. Can I get you anything?"

"No thanks," I said. And while he waited in line, I took a second to text my sister that Luca had just shown up, he was hot, and so far, seemed like a gentleman. Olivia made me promise to call as soon as I left.

When Luca returned with his coffee and a cheese Danish, I found myself feeling more excited for this date than I had about any of the others before it. He worked about two miles from the coffee shop as an investment advisor. "I've been with Millennium for a little over two years," he said. "It's been great so far. I can bring my dog to work."

"Seriously? I love dogs. What kind do you have?"

"A labradoodle named Chelsea."

I found myself leaning in a little as Luca talked, almost entranced by his clear blue eyes and the way his crisp button-down fit perfectly across his chest and shoulders. The man definitely worked out. Though thankfully not as much as Mick.

"Chelsea's a cute name for a dog. Where'd you come up with it?"

"Oh, I can't take credit for that. My girlfriend named her. She went to college in New York."

My eyes widened as I struggled to swallow the sip of tea I'd just taken. "I'm assuming you mean your *ex*-girlfriend?"

Luca looked genuinely confused. "No, Marybeth and I live together."

"You live together!"

"Oh, yeah, sorry. Is that a problem? Because it's not for Marybeth. She's cool with it."

"She's cool with you having online dating profiles and seeing other women?"

"Yeah. Or men. We identify as relationship queer." He sat back in his chair with an air of superiority. Like he and... Marybeth were somehow more progressive than me and my antiquated monogamist ideals.

"That's not even a real term." I would've laughed if my

current situation wasn't so sad.

Luca rolled his unfortunately gorgeous blue eyes. "That's exactly what someone who adheres to conventional norms of society would say. Marybeth and I don't subscribe to typical relationship roles. We're not monogamous or polyamorous or into bigamy or polygamy. We're just...whatever we want to be whenever we want to be it."

Despite my urge to get up and leave Luca sipping his Americano alone, this was all too strange not to investigate further. As a lawyer, I had no doubt met my share of unique or just plain weird individuals, especially during my internship with a high-profile defense attorney.

I was almost surprised I hadn't been able to sense something was off with him from the moment he sat down. But Luca seemed a different type of strange. He was a strange that usually stayed hidden until there was no avoiding revealing it—like a third nipple or a genital piercing.

"I'm pretty sure 'relationship queer' is offensive to the LGBTQ community," I said.

Luca laughed like the idea was ridiculous, like *I* was ridiculous. "I doubt that. They're an accepting group of people. Not subscribing to a particular belief regarding how relationships should be practiced is like not identifying with a particular gender. Genderqueer, *relationship* queer," he said like it was justification. "It's the same."

"It's not the same."

When Luca's phone sounded with a text, he picked it up and began typing back. "Sorry. One second. It's Marybeth wanting to know how everything's going."

I slumped back in my seat, wondering—and kind of hating myself for it—what Luca was writing back.

Fifteen minutes later, he left after telling me it wasn't going the way he planned. *No fucking kidding!* My sister was going to get an earful about this one.

"He told me he was 'relationship queer,' Liv. I think I've earned a break from this adventure for a while." I finished the last few sips of my tea and then spun the cup in my fingers.

I could tell by my sister's deflated sigh that she was disappointed, and I felt bad, but I couldn't keep going out with guys like the ones I'd met so far.

"I think you're being too picky," Olivia said.

"Not agreeing to see someone again after they tell you they have a girlfriend at home is *not* being too picky. Just like it wasn't being picky to turn down that date with the guy who said I was hot because I looked like his mother when she was young." That had actually been one of the less odd things he'd said. "It's called self-preservation. I could've ended up as a mummified corpse somewhere while he strutted around in my clothes."

"I feel like that's a reference to something, but I have no idea what."

"You're so young," I said with a shake of my head that my sister obviously couldn't see from the other end of the line.

Despite the almost ten-year age difference between us, we had been close since Olivia was born—and closer after our parents' deaths eight years ago. How could we not be when we only had each other to rely on?

I hadn't hesitated to take custody of my teenage sister, even though it meant putting my own life on hold for a bit. I'd been focused on raising Liv and finishing my law degree and eventually pursuing my career. But I'd never focused on myself—not from a purely selfish standpoint anyway.

"And you're old," Liv joked. "I need some nieces and nephews running around my new apartment, and soon your eggs are gonna expire."

"It's been lovely talking to you, sis. Gotta go, though."

"Wait!" Liv said. "I'm kidding. Well, sort of. I do want you to find someone soon. You deserve to find a guy who'll tell you how beautiful you are and cook you dinner after you've worked all day. Someone who'll make love to you with a passion that—"

"I'm hanging up now," I said, making Liv laugh, which thankfully caused her to stop talking about my imaginary sex life. Not like there was a *real* one to speak of.

"Love you, Lala." *Lala* was what Liv used to call me when she was learning to talk, and she still employed it from time to time when she was trying to prevent me from killing her.

"Love you too," I said before ending the call and tossing my phone in my bag. I waited another minute before standing to throw my trash away.

"Sorry. I know it's none of my business, but you definitely made the right call getting rid of the psycho."

I turned toward the direction of the voice, which belonged to a man who'd been sitting a few tables away. I'd noticed him on his laptop when I was waiting for Luca to arrive but hadn't paid him much attention until now. Though maybe I should have.

Even though he was seated, I could tell he was tall—long arms, broad shoulders, a swimmer's build with sandy-brown hair and eyes so green, they rivaled freshly cut grass on a spring afternoon.

"Oh, yeah, that guy was out there for sure. Who in their right mind thinks they can get someone to agree to date them when they already have a girlfriend?"

He raised his eyebrows in amusement. "It's ballsy, no doubt about that. But I was actually talking about the future Norman Bates."

I laughed. "Oh right, *that* psycho."

"And I wasn't trying to eavesdrop on your phone conversation. I sometimes pick up what happens in the background without meaning to. I've never been much of a music guy while I work. I start singing along, and before I know it, I've either accomplished nothing at all or worked every line of the latest Taylor Swift song into my doodling."

"Didn't peg you for a Swifty," I said.

He shrugged. "I'm a sucker for anything with a catchy beat." He gave me a little wave. "I'm Grayson, by the way."

"Nice to meet you, Grayson. I'm Isla."

This story continues in *Misadventures with a Sexpert*!

ACKNOWLEDGMENTS

First and foremost, I must thank my awesome wife, Jessica. Wearing a drab olive jacket and a toothy smile, she wandered into a donut shop one evening. With her big blond hair, height-challenged frame, and perfectly applied makeup, she scanned the establishment, looking for a place to sit down. A real-life biker who'd recently been released from federal prison offered her a seat. She took a chance and sat next to the tattooed hooligan. We are now living our happily ever after together, in Naples, Florida.

Additionally, I'd like to give mention to my mother, Anita Hildreth. Her lifelong passion has been to be a writer, but she's never taken the time to pursue her dreams. She's expressed pride in me for doing so and encouraged me to continue when things were bleak. Thank you, Mom, for being you.

My late father, David Hildreth, was a former marine and a man's man. He cried upon reading my first book. At the time, I couldn't recall ever seeing him cry. The tears he shed and the words he spoke as a result of that novel fueled me to continue my quest to publish a book traditionally. Thanks, Pop. I hope I've made you proud.

My brother and late sister also deserve thanks for simply putting up with me for all these years. *tips hat* Thanks, you two, for never giving up on me (when many would have).

To my six children who have sacrificed so much as I work countless hours polishing my manuscripts, I can't help but offer a heartfelt thank you. The missed time together, the cancelled trips to the beach, and the days that you waited for me to finish one more chapter—only to find out that it wasn't complete until long after you went to bed—I must apologize for. Erin, Alec, Derek, Landon, Lily, and Charlee, you are my world. It may not always seem like it, but you are.

Without the encouragement of my former employer, David Bowlin, I never would have begun to write. He provided the means for me to pen my first book. Dave, I can't thank you enough. It seems you've stepped into my life on each occasion when things aren't as they should be, providing guidance along a path much more desirable than the one I've chosen. Thank you isn't enough, but it's all I have.

Lastly, to Meredith Wild. Thank you for taking the chance. To the editor, Scott Saunders, I extend my hand. Thank you. I'm not the easiest author to work with, and you did so with a professional posture that didn't include any requests that I took exception to. You're a class act, sir.

For now, that's all I've got.

Until next time...

MORE MISADVENTURES

**VISIT MISADVENTURES.COM
FOR MORE INFORMATION!**

ABOUT THE AUTHOR

Born in San Diego, California, Scott now calls Naples, Florida, home. Residing along the Gulf Coast with his wife, Jessica, and six children, he somehow finds twelve hours a day to work on his writing. A hybrid author who has self-published more than three-dozen romance and erotica novels, his three-book Mafia Made series with Harlequin is his first venture into the world of traditionally published works but certainly won't be his last.

Scott has spent his entire life pushing boundaries, and his writing is no exception. Addicted to riding his Harley-Davidson, tattoos, and drinking coffee, he can generally be found in a tattoo shop, on his Harley, or in a local coffee house when not writing.

Loyal to the fans and faithful followers who allowed him to make writing a full-time career, Scott communicates with his followers on Facebook almost daily. He encourages his readers to follow him on Facebook and Twitter.